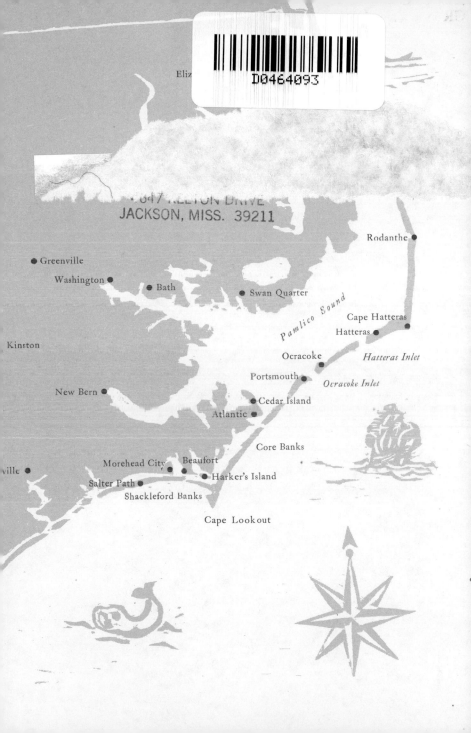

Eliz

Rodanthe

Greenville

Washington

Bath

Swan Quarter

Pamlico Sound

Cape Hatteras

Hatteras

Kinston

Ocracoke

Hatteras Inlet

Portsmouth

Ocracoke Inlet

New Bern

Cedar Island

Atlantic

Core Banks

Morehead City   Beaufort

ville

Harker's Island

Salter Path

Shackleford Banks

Cape Lookout

The Flaming Ship
of Ocracoke

By *Charles Harry Whedbee*

The Flaming Ship of Ocracoke

& Other Tales of the Outer Banks

Illustrated by Virginia Ingram

JOHN F. BLAIR, *Publisher*
Winston-Salem, North Carolina

Copyright © 1971 by JOHN F. BLAIR, *Publisher*
Library of Congress Catalog Card Number: 76–156458
ISBN 0–910244–61–8

Second Printing, 1971

Printed in the United States of America
by Heritage Printers, Inc.
Charlotte, North Carolina

To
Frances & Will

Foreword

In those golden years before civilization had too much touched the North Carolina Outer Banks, there existed on these ocean shores a sort of latter-day Garden of Eden of sun, sea, and sand. For the young, it was a never-never land of excitement and a time of seemingly endless summer days. And there was so much more that permeated this place that one could not touch or smell— the legends, lore, folk memory. It filled the summer visitor with a strange sense of wonder and mystery, though the Bankers themselves accepted it all as a very real and integral part of their lives.

Today, though great bridges span the various sounds, connecting these once-isolated islands with the mainland, and concrete highways thread their busy ways over the bleached white sand, the memories and legends still persist as part and parcel of the native Bankers' lives and land.

Some five years ago this writer ventured hesitantly into print with a small volume entitled *Legends of the Outer Banks and Tar Heel Tidewater*, hoping to capture some of the mystery and flavor of these memories for the reading public. Since that time, several other equally interesting folk tales have been recalled, some evoked by the reminiscences of old friends and others by the natural stirrings of folk memory.

So, once more, this writer ventures hesitantly into the world of the printed word, hoping that these newly recorded tales may be preserved in this small volume for the interested reader's enjoyment and enlightenment. As

FOREWORD

in the earlier volume, some of these stories are true. Some contain no more than, maybe, a germ of truth or a spark of native islander wisdom. But, in the words of one who lived many years ago on this magic strand and dearly loved the ways and beliefs of its often heroic people, it can only be said:

> I do not say what I know to be,
> I only tell what was told to me.

CHARLES HARRY WHEDBEE

Whalebone Junction
Nag's Head, North Carolina

Contents

The Flaming Ship
of Ocracoke

The Duel at Hammock House

*During the late sixteen hundreds, the lovely coastal set-*tlement of Beaufort Town was already an established port. Most of the coastwise sailing ships made use of the fine, safe harbor, and for many it was a regular port-of-call. It was common knowledge among the skippers who were experienced in navigating this harbor that, in order to sail through the harbor entrance safely, one had to take sight bearings on the large hammock, or knoll, which was the dominant piece of high ground on the shore. When a skipper could get an unobstructed sighting on the hammock from outside the inlet, he could set his course directly for it and gain safe passage through the shoals of the harbor entrance.

Thus, it seems quite natural that, today, there stands a beautiful dwelling, known as Hammock House, which was built hundreds of years ago atop that Beaufort Town hammock by a group of owner-captains who regularly came to port there. It served as a sort of club, or home away from home, for these men of the sea.

No one knows exactly how old Hammock House really is, but there are records that seem to indicate that it was already built and in use by the year 1703. It was built from materials supplied by the captain-owners, which they gathered from all over the world. It stood on a foundation of white oak timbers from the banks of the River Clyde near Dumbarton, Scotland. There was an abundance of mahogany, teakwood, cypress, rosewood, sandlewood, and heart of pine. The fittings were of copper and brass. It was constructed as a graceful, three-story structure with large chimneys on both ends, a fireplace in every room, and deep, shady porches on the second floor, as well as on the first. The front of the house faced Beaufort Inlet, and from the second-story porch there was a magnificent view of the inlet and for miles to seaward. Less than twenty feet from the front of the house, a pier served as a mooring place for "pulling boats," and a driveway for coaches circled the rear of the house.

The house today is as solid as it was then, though there are no inhabitants living in it—at least no human inhabitants. The children of the area are strictly cautioned to give a wide berth to the house because, to this day, some very strange things happen there. The bloodstains on the stairway defy even the most sophisticated detergents, and some people tell of mysterious lights which flit from room to room on occasion. Neighbors whisper about the hoarse cries and the clashing of steel, as though men were engaged in mortal combat.

There is an explanation for all this in a story, which the old-timers will swear is true. It begins in a time when Hammock House had already attained the reputation of being the height of luxury and elegance of the day. More captains bought into the venture, and the succession of balls and other lavish entertainment seemed never-ending. According to historians, it was the dream of all coastwise captains to have a "membership" in Hammock House, for admission was gained only by invitation.

One of the owner-members of Hammock House was an ambitious young captain named Madison Brothers. He was known as a hard-driving and demanding captain, who had "come up through the fo'c'sle." That is, he had made his own way by hard work from the job of cabin boy to the position of owner, as well as captain, of his own fine vessel. An excellent seaman and a good business-man, he had one very serious personality defect, an ungovernable temper. His fits of rage, particularly when he was drinking, were well known; people took care not to provoke him. It was whispered that he had killed more than once in anger but always in a fair fight. Soon his given name began to be shortened by those who knew him, and instead of Madison Brothers, he was called Captain "Mad" Brothers.

Captain Mad must have had a gentler side to his nature, too, because he wooed and won a beautiful young Baltimore lady named Samantha Ashby. Although he was considerably older than she, the Captain must have convinced her of his sincerity and the depth of his ardor. She consented to become his bride, and plans for the wedding were made.

These were to be no ordinary nuptials. Miss Ashby was the orphaned daughter of a fine old Baltimore family, and Captain Brothers was determined that the wedding should be done in style. In those days, it was the very height of fashion to have a wedding performed in the famous Hammock House, so it was agreed that Samantha and Mad would be married there by the Anglican minister of Beaufort Town. In deference to the proprieties, Miss Ashby was to travel to Beaufort by stagecoach with her entourage of chaperones and bridal attendants, while Captain Brothers was to sail his ship down the coast and meet her in Beaufort Town. After the wedding, they were to take their honeymoon aboard his fine ship on a cruise to the British West Indies.

Stagecoach and ship left Baltimore on the same day and headed southward. The coach made exceptionally good time and rolled merrily over the dusty, rutted post road toward the wedding rendezvous. Not so Captain Brothers' ship. It was one day out of port when the first mate was taken desperately ill. The Captain's medicine chest was not equal to the emergency, and he had to "wear ship" and return to port, where the then delirious officer was put ashore and carried to a hospital. This took another full day.

Now two days late and shorthanded as well, Mad Brothers once again put to sea and once again ran into the kind of bad luck that sometimes plagues a voyage. An inexperienced helmsman broke a forestay during a sudden and violent squall, and the foremast came toppling down, carrying rigging and stays with it. Once again the ship was hove to, and the long, tedious task of cutting and chopping away the wreckage and rigging a jury foremast began. To add to the difficulties, both wind and sea began increasing by the hour. It seemed, to Mad, that the devil was sitting cross-legged for him.

In Beaufort, meanwhile, the stagecoach carrying the wedding party arrived right on time. Of course, arrangements had been made beforehand, and the newcomers were welcomed in style. The luxurious accommodations of Hammock House were made available for the delight of the members of the wedding party. All of the travelers had heard of the famous place, but most of them had never seen it before, and it more than lived up to their fondest hopes. Several sea captains and their wives were in residence at the time, and much excitement and anticipation prevailed. Although no word had been received about Captain Brothers, he was too skilled a seaman to warrant any worry about his safety. It was assumed that he was just delayed by adverse weather.

A most pleasant surprise was in store for Samantha Ashby that very first evening after her arrival. A formal dance had been arranged, and the officers of several ships lying in Beaufort Harbor had been invited. Unknown to Samantha, one of the ships in harbor was the British warship *H. M. S. Diligent*, and one of her junior officers was Samantha's brother, Lieutenant Carruthers Ashby.

What a joyous and unexpected surprise for both these young people when they came face to face in that ballroom! Mail delivery being an uncertain thing in those days, he had not heard of her approaching marriage, and she had not known in what part of the world he was serving. Samantha was completely happy at this joyous reunion.

For the next several days Lieutenant Ashby came ashore every afternoon, and he and his sister took long walks about Beaufort Town and talked, bringing each other up to date on happenings since they had last been together. The loss of both their parents had brought these two closer to each other than most brothers and sisters, even though his profession kept them apart for long periods of time. One of their favorite places to sit and talk was the old burying ground in Beaufort, with its green grass and its huge live oaks bending low to the ground. There they would sit, for hours on end, recalling happy memories of their childhood. These were golden days for them both, and Lieutenant Ashby helped to ease Samantha's growing concern about the safety of her betrothed.

At sea, Captain Brothers was making heavy weather of it. With his ship limping along under makeshift rigging and under an unfavorable wind, he was literally fit to be tied. He had already vented his temper on the hides of two of his crew, and it seemed that nothing would go right for him. For the last two days he had been hitting the bottle with regularity and was working himself into a towering rage at the world and everybody in it.

It was dusk when he finally rounded Cape Lookout and turned his ship toward the entrance of Beaufort Harbor. As the width of the inlet opened before him, he gazed impatiently through a powerful telescope in the direction of Hammock House. To his surprise, he saw lights ablaze in every window. Obviously a gay party was under way, whether the bridegroom was present or not. So they were not at all worried by his lateness! To his burning impatience and drunken confusion were now added waves of unreasoning self-pity and a growing suspicion of every body in that house.

Roaring profanities, he ordered the captain's gig lowered over the side just as soon as the ship's anchor had struck the bottom of Beaufort Harbor. Even in his condition, the Captain was able to slide expertly down the lines still attached to the gig from the ship's davits. Once in the pulling boat, he settled himself unsteadily in its stern, as two members of his crew strained at the oars to set him ashore. The oarsmen looked more like a boarding party than a bridegroom's escort, for they had large horse pistols thrust in their belts and wicked-looking case knives sheathed on their hips. When you served under the Mad Captain, you were wise to be prepared for any eventuality.

In Hammock House, the huge crystal chandelier in the main ballroom had been lighted, and the orchestra was striking up the first tune of the evening. On the first-floor veranda, the beautiful young bride-to-be and her brother strolled in the soft evening dusk with their arms around each others' waists. As usual, their talk was of their childhood and of shared memories. As she finished a particularly tender reminiscence, Samantha turned her wistfully smiling face up to her brother's, and, in a wave of brotherly love, he stooped and kissed her cheek.

At that very instant, Captain Mad Brothers stormed up the three low steps onto the dimly lit veranda of Hammock House.

"Betrayed!" he roared, and sprang to attack the young officer. Drawing his cutlass from its sheath, he fell to in a determined effort to cleave the young man's head. Lieutenant Ashby was armed only with an *épée*, a dueling sword with a triangular blade which was popular with the young officers of the day. He was an expert with it and nimbly defended himself against the Captain's first bull-like charge, though he instantly sensed the identity of his assailant.

All might yet have ended well, because the other captains then converged toward the duelers to separate them, but Brothers' two crewmen blocked their way with leveled and cocked pistols.

"Affair of honor. Let them be," warned the pistoleers, and the would-be peacemakers could see that they meant business. Their cries of protest went unheeded.

On the duel went, with slash and parry and riposte, with lunge and retreat and disengage and lunge again, all up and down the length of the ballroom, and finally up the stairs, as Lieutenant Ashby backed away and sought the advantage of height. Up and up they fought, with the younger swordsman always on the defensive and calling on his adversary to desist and listen to explanations. Finally Captain Brothers backed his opponent up the stairs which led to the third floor. Here the young officer had to make his stand, because there was no more room for retreat. As he lunged down the stairs to press a counter-attack, his foot slipped, and he fell headlong toward his attacker.

Quicker than the strike of a barracuda, Captain Brothers' left hand flashed toward his left hip and whipped out the long, razor-sharp case knife sheathed there. Upward he struck with the knife toward the falling body of the lieutenant. With deadly accuracy, he buried the knife to the hilt in his victim's chest, inflicting a fatal wound. The weight of the falling body carried both antagonists to the floor at the foot of the stairs.

As soon as he could disentangle himself from his mortally wounded opponent, Captain Brothers motioned his two crewmen to his side. Under cover of their leveled guns, they retreated to their gig and, in that craft, to the ship. Anchor was immediately hoisted, and the ship fled back through Beaufort Inlet and out to sea. Apparently no effort was made to stop them, and history is silent as to whether Captain Brothers ever found out whom he had killed and whether he was ever hunted down and made to pay for his crime.

Every effort was made to save Lieutenant Ashby. His ship's surgeon and the local doctors did their best, but the wound was too severe; he died in Hammock House that same night.

It is told that, before he died, Lieutenant Ashby made a strange last request. He begged that, if he died, he be buried standing upright, in his full dress uniform, facing southward toward Beaufort Inlet and the open sea beyond. Tradition has it that both these requests were carried out. It is certain that, to this day, you may find the grave of a young British naval officer in Beaufort Burying Ground who was, indeed, buried standing at attention. Of course, there are those who say that it is another British naval officer buried here, one who died of yellow fever in Beaufort. Legend persists, however, that the grave is really the resting place of Lieutenant Ashby.

Hammock House itself still stands, as beautiful and as architecturally sound as ever. Its windows still look out over Beaufort Inlet as though brooding over the wild events that took place in its past. The bloodstains are still on the upper stairs, and they are particularly noticeable when the weather becomes damp or foggy. The sounds of laughter and sweet music still come and go and, on occasion, the clangor of that battle of long, long ago. People who know about such things will assure you that this is true. A goodly number of highly intelligent people believe it with all their hearts. So do a number of adventurous children of Beaufort Town who did not heed their parents' warnings to stay away from Hammock House.

The Flaming Ship of Ocracoke

Some most unusual things continue to happen just off the northern shore of Ocracoke Inlet. Of course, this region is known the world over as a part of the Graveyard of the Atlantic, and many are the tales of shipwrecks and

13

sailors lost at sea and of treasures lying buried beneath the shifting sands of Diamond Shoals. Most of these legends have no recurring manifestations; but the Ocracoke Happening, they say, repeats itself year after year, always under the same conditions and always at the same spot. Many people have seen it time after time, and always on the night when the new moon makes its first appearance in September. Thus, the dates may differ from year to year, but that sliver of new moon is always part of the scene.

In the region itself, the most widely accepted explanation is a combination of history and folk memory which has been told and retold by the older fishermen to their sons and grandsons. Many of these old-timers may not be able to name the current Secretary of the Interior, but they can tell you, with amazing accuracy, of the time when Anne was Queen of England and many efforts were being made to colonize the Carolinas. This was a time when the continent of Europe was in a ferment. The tiny German Palatinate had been overrun, time and again, by the vicious wars between Catholic and Protestant armies. The people were weary with so-called religious wars, and they longed for peace.

In the beautiful Rhine River Valley in 1689, the retreating armies of Louis XIV had brutally scourged and laid waste the entire countryside, leaving everything destroyed and most of the people destitute. Some ten thousand Palatines, as they were called, flooded into England for refuge, and the authorities did not know what to do with them. No beggars, these, but honest and skilled craftsmen, miners, and artisans of the first order. Such an influx of jobless thousands threw the British economy completely out of kilter.

The British people, though sympathetic at first, soon began to complain, so the English Queen listened with favor when the Swiss Baron Christopher de Graffenried, eager to mend his own personal fortunes and to solve the problems of many of the Palatines at the same time, proposed taking several hundred of these poor people to the Province of Carolina in the New World across the sea. England desperately needed colonists, and the Palatines just as desperately needed new homes, so Queen Anne told de Graffenried to go ahead with his plan.

The mass migration, organized and directed by the good baron, was beset by trials and tribulations, but it finally resulted in the settlement of a large portion of land in what is now eastern North Carolina. The settlement was known, at first, by the Indian name Chattoka. Today it is identified as the beautiful city of New Bern (formerly New Berne). Many people know of these fine Swiss and German folk who have meant so much to the history of North Carolina and of their leader, Baron de Graffenried, the Landgrave of Carolina.

Most people, though, do not know about a later shipload of Palatines whose financial status was much better but whose destiny was not to be so bright. While homeless, they were still possessed of a large amount of gold and silver plate, gold candlesticks, and many valuable coins and jewels, which they had managed to conceal from invading armies. Whereas the earlier Palatines had come to America by means of financing furnished by the British government, these later emigrants paid for their own passage by subscription among themselves. They, too, were looking for a new and better home in Carolina. They had heard good reports of the colony from their friends who had come over with de Graffenried and were eager to make their own beginnings in that new land.

The passage from England was uneventful, as day followed sunny day, and the ship made good time. The hopes of these thrifty Palatines were high as they looked forward to soon joining their countrymen in New Berne. Each of them had been very careful to conceal his precious possessions in the sea bags and chests allowed in the sleeping quarters below decks. So far as could be seen, they were just as poor as their friends who had come before them.

At that time, Ocracoke Inlet was the principal point of entry for ships with passengers or cargoes bound for the interior of North Carolina. Ocean-going vessels could negotiate the inlet and sail over the shallow sounds to the inland cities, or they could, and usually did, anchor just inside or outside the inlet and transfer the passengers or cargoes to smaller boats which were bound for New Berne, Bath, or Edenton. Travelers were usually given a few hours in which to stretch their legs and walk about in Portsmouth Town before beginning the final lap of their journey.

Thus it was with the ship carrying these later Palatines. They arrived offshore before dawn and anchored in the calm waters just to the seaward from Ocracoke Inlet. The passengers were in a fever of excitement. Lights could be seen from the houses on the nearby shore, and the smell of woodsmoke from the early morning cooking fires in Pilot Town (now called Ocracoke Village) carried across the water to the pilgrims. The children were the most enthusiastic of all as they ran back and forth on the deck, laughing and playing. The perilous sea voyage was over, and they were now only a short distance from their new homes.

Among the adults, there was more sober talk of Indians and whether or not they would continue to be friendly, of gold mines, and of the prospect of living without the constant threat of war. It was a time of new beginnings. They believed that they had, at last, found a fresh page on which to write their own personal histories.

By the time it was fully daylight, all the Palatines were dressed in their best clothes and were assembled on the deck of the ship. They were eager to set foot on land and to see the sights of Portsmouth Town. Not wanting to risk the theft of their valuables, they made the mistake of bringing these belongings up on deck with them. There they stood, their eyes full of hope and anticipation and their hands full of more treasure than the ship's captain had ever seen in any one place in his entire lifetime.

Unknown to his passengers, the Captain had, at one time, been a pirate, but he had taken the "King's Pardon," promising to lead a law-abiding life. At the sight of the Palatines' treasure, however, his new moral code promptly went by the board. Calling a hurried meeting with his officers and then an even briefer meeting with his crew, the skipper found them all of a like mind to his. This was too easy a chance to be missed.

So the plot was laid. The Captain told his passengers

that there had been some delay in arranging their transportation to New Berne, but he promised to take care of that by the next morning. He advised them to return to their quarters below decks and to get some rest against the rigors of the next stage of their travels, as they would not be able to go ashore until the next day. This the Palatines did, taking their belongings with them, not even questioning the fact that the Captain had waved away several small boats and lighters which had come out to get the business of taking the passengers and their belongings ashore.

The night that followed was the first night of the new moon in that September of long ago. The sun had set some hours before, and the new moon was low in the sky when the crew, led by the Captain and both mates, slipped up behind the few passengers still taking the air on deck and silently strangled them with short lengths of line. Then, silently and swiftly, they crept below, knives in hand, and cut the throats of every remaining passenger, children as well as adults. Not one was spared.

These brutal murders accomplished, the crew then brought lights into the hold and methodically ripped open all the sea bags and chests belonging to the murdered people, stealing all the gold, silver, jewels, and coins they had so much coveted on the deck of the ship that morning. Pirate-like, they divided their loot on the deck of the ship. Then, lowering the ship's longboat into the sea, they prepared to go ashore. Just before they left the ship, they spread the vessel's mainsail and jib and slipped the anchor chain so that the craft could run before the gentle southwest wind. As a final touch, the Captain set fire to the large pile of rifled sea bags and chests which had been heaped near the mainmast. This was to make more credible the tale of disaster they intended to tell when they reached the shore.

About halfway to shore, the men rested on their oars and looked back at the ship. The Captain turned his head, too, and saw that the fire had spread more rapidly than he had anticipated. Apparently the lines holding the furled topsails and topgallantsails to the yard had burned in two. Now, all the sails seemed to be set, and the ship was driving at full speed, not in a northeasterly direction but almost due west, right toward the crowded longboat.

The sails seemed to be solid sheets of flame, and from the hold of the burning ship came long, loud, pitiful wails, filling the dark sea with the mournful sound of souls in torment. The inferno ship bore down upon the frantically fleeing longboat until, with a crash of splintering timbers, it rolled the doomed little craft over and over under its keel, spilling the murderer-robbers into the sea. Most of them were drowned outright. Some, however, were able to cling to pieces of wreckage from the longboat until they were washed ashore many hours later. Amazingly, the burning death ship then came about and, with no living soul at her lashed helm, set a steady course toward the northeast again, her sails still aflame and the mournful wails still emanating from the hold.

To this day, they say, that flaming ship reappears on the first night of the new moon in September. Her sails are always sheets of flame and her rigging glows red-hot in the near darkness. Always there is the accompanying eerie wailing, as she sails swiftly and purposefully toward the northeast. Three times she runs her ghostly course on each occasion. She always seems to sail from the water just offshore to a point where she can barely be seen as a small glow on the distant horizon. They say she will sail out of sight; and then, twice again, she will suddenly reappear just offshore and sail toward the northeast. Those who have seen her say you can always smell the odor of burning canvas and hemp, and she always moves northeastward, regardless of the direction and velocity of the wind.

So far as is known, not one single piece of the treasure belonging to the doomed Palatines has ever been washed up on the beach. So far as can be told, the flaming ship will continue to sail her fiery course each year while those betrayed pilgrims continue to look for peace and happiness in that new home to which they came so near.

Pin Hill

Just south of Jockey's Ridge at Nag's Head is the gently rounded, graceful sand dune called Engagement Hill, so named because of the many romances that have had their beginnings there. Just south of Engagement Hill lies an even lower dune that goes by the name of Pin Hill. These colorful place names are carried on most of the oldest maps of this section of the Outer Banks. They have been so known to generations of both visitors to, and natives of, the region.

The reason Pin Hill is so named is that for many years the dune has been literally filled with a great number of metallic straight pins of the type dressmakers use. For generations past and down to this good day, a visitor to the hill has had no difficulty in finding sheafs or rows of straight pins all rusted together until they resemble ornamental combs. Some of them seem to have been fused together by some great force such as lightning. You can look all afternoon and find a great number of these sheafs of straight pins and then go back in the morning and there are just as many there on the hill as before. It is as if you had not removed a single pin.

Most of the attempted explanations of this phenomenon have to do with the supposition that some pin salesman lost a shipment of straight pins. If this is the reason, that shipment certainly must have been unusually large to have lasted, now, for generations. Another explanation is based on the fact that many years ago a hostelry named the Toney House was located very near the hill, and the pins could have come from that hotel. Very plausible indeed, but why such an enormous supply of straight pins in a hotel? And why do they continue to be found to this very day, just as if the supply were constantly being replenished? The most satisfactory and most interesting explanation seems to be one told by a very old man who, at one time, ran another hotel near the spot.

Back in the early eighteen hundreds there were several windmills down on Hatteras Island. They were placed there for the same reason that later brought the Wright Brothers to Kill Devil Hill. That is the reliable, steady breeze. These windmills were built on spindles, or pivots, similar to the way some Dutch windmills are built. The whole structure could be turned to face whatever direction the wind was blowing from. Usually they ground corn, which was brought over from the mainland in boats. The miller took some of his pay in the resultant corn meal. This windmill business was, normally, only a supplement to his regular vocation of fishing. The operator would use his fishing boat to take his meal up to the settlements along the Outer Banks for sale or trade. The tall structures must have made very picturesque additions to the scenery of the coastline. They certainly must have served also as landmarks for the fishing boats offshore.

One of these industrious mill operators was an honest fisherman named Christopher Columbus Midgett, who lived with his wife in a little shingled cottage near his windmill on the Pamlico Sound shore of Hatteras Island. Close by the house, there was a very low place in the terrain. This had formerly been a mullet pond, a place where fishermen sometimes dumped their fish to keep them alive until they were ready to sell or use them. This pond had gone dry many years before and now was only a saucer-like depression in the sand except when an occasional storm tide filled it with water to a depth of a few inches.

On a summer evening in 1830, a sudden, violent squall line developed in the sound, with winds of near hurricane force blowing directly onto the beach from the open sound. The storm in itself was not so unusual. What was unusual about it was that it caught a herd of porpoises totally unprepared and cavorting too near the shore line for their safety. By next morning, fully half the herd had been blown, not only ashore, but over the beach and into the old mullet pond, which was now half full of water.

The porpoises were only partly submerged, and they thrashed about like miniature whales, half in and half out of the water. The rest of the herd milled about anxiously just offshore, unable to help their stranded fellows but standing by, nevertheless. Now beached porpoises are pitiful things. They breathe air instead of water and are in no danger of suffocating, but they are water creatures and will soon die if not returned to their native habitat or, at least, kept constantly wet so that their skin does not dry out and crack open. It is an infrequent thing for them to be caught in such a plight, as they are extremely weather-wise. When they are trapped, their pitiful cries sound very much like those of a baby and are a nerve-rending thing to hear.

Chris Midgett just could not bear to see these friendly beasts caught in so hopeless a situation. His good wife was "down the island" visiting relatives, and the other able-bodied men were out fishing, so he was all alone. He had planned to spend the day in catching up with his milling, but now his conscience would not let him do that. Pulling lustily on the wheeled counterweight, he revolved the turret of his windmill until the big sails no longer caught the wind, and the mill coasted to a stop. Tying down the sails so they could not accidentally begin to revolve again, he left the mill with a large lot of corn yet unground. He

seized his short-handled, square-bladed spade and frantically began to dig a channel from the mullet pond to the
sound. If he could just finish it in time, there would be
enough tidewater to float the imprisoned porpoises back
to the waters of Pamlico Sound. He knew that the other
porpoises would help the refugees find the safety of nearby deep-water sloughs. If he missed the flood of the next
high tide, tomorrow might be too late.

Most coast dwellers, whether highly educated or un-
schooled, have a high respect and admiration for porpoises. They feel almost a kinship with these extremely
intelligent and friendly animals. The instances of porpoises befriending humans are many. To Midgett, they
had long seemed to be almost brothers, and he was determined to rescue this segment of the porpoise community
if it was within his power to do so. It seemed to him that
the free porpoises out in the sound actually knew what
he was attempting. They swam back and forth excitedly
and made frantic whistling noises, which he took to be
encouragement and urging.

All day long he labored at his back-breaking work, not
even stopping for his midday meal. By sunset, and with
the help of an unusually high and strong tide, he opened
the escape route. Slowly, in single file, and with much
help from Chris, the porpoises finally made their way to
open water. There they lay, backs just awash, breathing
in a labored way through the blowholes in the tops of their
heads as they rested and regained their strength. Not a
single individual of the waiting herd departed until each
of the rescued ones had regained his strength and moved
under his own power out into deeper water.

Under the powerful pull of the tide, the water from the sound moved into the mullet pond, flooding it full before receding with a rush through Chris Midgett's ditch as the tide fell. Once again the mullet pond was only a damp, saucer-like depression in the sand. Now, there was a dry, shallow trench leading back into Pamlico Sound from the former prison. The rescue had been made in the nick of time. Already the wind was beginning to refill the ditch with dry sand. In a comparatively short time, it would be covered over again. There would soon be no tangible sign of the miller's heroic and unselfish labor except, maybe, that large pile of unground corn still waiting in the mill.

Christopher Midgett was exhausted. He had labored frantically all day long under a blazing sun, and every muscle in his tired body ached with pain. He trudged to his little cottage, pulled off part of his clothes, and fell into bed. In no time at all he was fast asleep.

The miller-fisherman dreamed a very realistic dream. He dreamed that he awoke sometime after midnight to find his bedroom suffused with a sort of phosphorescent glow. Standing at the foot of his bed, trident in hand and gazing directly at him, was Poseidon, the ancient King of the Sea. The source of the eerie, white light could not be detected by Christopher, but it seemed to surround Poseidon and beam outward from him to all the corners of the room.

In slow and stately language, which seemed to have in it the cadence of the rolling sea, the Sea King spoke of his pleasure and his gratitude for Midgett's labor. Observing that such unselfish acts should be rewarded, the phosphorescent visitor promised the astounded miller that his recompense would be forthcoming.

Handing Midgett a ring set with a glowing pearl, which was fully the size of an English walnut, he boomed, "In ancient and honored fashion, you shall be granted any three wishes your heart desires. Take this ring as a means of communication with me, and when you have decided what your wishes shall be, only rub the ring with the thumb of your right hand, and I shall reappear to hear your command." Then, suddenly, he was gone, and the room was dark. Only the huge pearl glowed with a sort of soft inner fire. The little miller then dreamed that he fell fast asleep.

When he awoke the next morning, he thought wistfully of his dream. If only such a thing could be true! As he straightened his bed and smoothed the covers, his hand ran idly under his pillow. His entire body tightened with surprise as his fingers closed around a hard object that filled his palm. It was the ring—Poseidon's ring! It was not a dream, after all; he had the delightful prospect of, not one, but three wishes for anything that he might desire.

When Christopher's wife Mary returned that next day, he told her all that had transpired. Her doubts vanished at the sight of the beautiful ring, and, as excited as children, they took counsel as to what they should wish for. They soon agreed that untold wealth was not a suitable wish, as it would, in all likelihood, bring only care and worry. At least, most of the rich people they had seen had not appeared very carefree, and they had no desire to leave their home island.

Eventually Christopher and Mary wisely decided that they should spend their wishes on something more lasting than money and more rewarding than fame. They were very simple people, but they possessed a native wisdom that gave them a very clear-eyed and true sense of values.

Rubbing the giant pearl with his thumb, Christopher summoned the Sea God as directed and wished, first, for a long, healthy, and contented life for his wife Mary. As his second wish, he asked for the same thing for himself. He and Mary never doubted the depth and permanence of their love. The thing they wanted most of all was the very maximum number of years together, in good health, to share and express that love. All else was secondary.

Poseidon gladly granted both wishes and warned that only one wish remained. He also reminded them that, if Midgett lost the ring, the finder would have the same power to demand and receive the third wish that Christopher would have had. The ring was negotiable and was to be guarded with great care. On looking at the ring after their visitor had departed, it seemed to Chris that the pearl was greatly reduced in size since the granting of the two wishes.

By the next week, the mill's share of ground corn meal had accumulated to a large amount, so Christopher decided to travel in his little sailboat up the sound to dispose of his product. It was his custom to sell a part of the meal for cash money and to trade the rest for other things Mary needed to keep house. After brief stops at the little sound-side villages on Hatteras, he made his first major call at Nag's Head. Here, as was his custom, he planned to stay overnight at the Toney House. This was a very nice inn, and the operators gladly took his fine quality meal as payment for his lodging.

Back in those days, there were itinerant merchants called pack peddlers who traveled, mostly on foot, all over the Outer Banks and elsewhere. They sold all kinds of items from huge packs or bags which they carried on their backs. These merchants would have yard goods, pots and pans, pins and needles and thread, patent medicines of all kinds, and even fishhooks and bottle stoppers. Most of these pack peddlers were honest merchants, who filled a very real need of the time and region. A few of them, however, were blackguards and thieves, who would rob and cheat and steal whenever they thought they could get away with it.

One of this latter kind of peddler was also staying at the Toney House and had just about finished his round of the homes in the little settlement on the day Christopher Midgett arrived. This man was very methodical. He had four pouches—white, black, green, and brown—which he used for keeping separate his fishhooks, pins, needles, and money. The pouches provided easy storage in his huge back pack and ready access when needed. Being of a very suspicious nature, like most untrustworthy people, he frequently shifted his merchandise and his money from pouch to pouch just in case someone had noticed him taking money from one particular pouch and had conceived the idea of stealing that pouch.

It was inevitable that all the guests at an inn like the Toney House should meet each other, and the pack peddler and Christopher soon became acquainted. After seeing the little miller make several sales for cash, the peddler tried to devise some scheme whereby he could relieve his fellow lodger of some of his hard-earned money. This coastal bumpkin should not be too hard to bilk, the peddler thought, and besides, it was time for him to move on.

After supper that night, the peddler was successful in fast-talking Midgett into a drinking session. Christopher was really living it up, for he was excited over his recent good fortune, and his new-found friend seemed like a nice enough fellow. Unused as he was to hard liquor, the miller did not want to appear naive, so he very foolishly matched the peddler drink for drink until he became quite drunk.

Then the peddler talked Christopher into a round of gambling with cards the inn provided for the pleasure of its guests. He baited Christopher along, in the time-honored way, by letting him win several small sums. Then, moving in for the kill, he proceeded to win nearly everything Midgett had on him. The game proceeded with the drinking, and the bets became larger and larger. By then, the miller was practically broke except for his mysterious ring.

On several occasions, as the evening wore on, the peddler had noticed that ring as his opponent dipped into his money bag to feed his losses at the table. Finally, the peddler asked to see the ring and remarked on its eerie beauty. In his condition, the miller forgot his usual caution and proceeded to tell his companion all about the circumstances under which he had received the ring as well about its magical properties. Of course the crook sneered to himself about the magic powers of the pearl. It was a very pretty ring, though, and would probably bring a nice price in some city, he thought. So thinking, the bag merchant decided to trick his companion and make the ring his own.

Christopher Midgett was not an experienced tippler, but he was possessed of a fine, strong body as a result of a lifetime of clean living and hard, physical labor. This robust health and excellent physical condition gave him some capacity and tolerance for the whiskey they were consuming. While the pack peddler could and did drink him down, that schemer had to consume a great quantity of liquor to do so, and he could hardly have been classified as sober himself. Nevertheless, the peddler was still cunning enough to let the miller win a couple of rather big pots and then lose them right back, until he was again down to the point where he had almost nothing left except the ring.

The inevitable last game, with its inescapable final big bet, came to pass; all the peddler's winnings were wagered against the beautiful pearl ring, all on the turn of one card. And it was, of course, the peddler's deal. The result, while predictable, almost did not come off as planned. So intoxicated was the peddler that he had difficulty in palming the card he wanted to turn. Anyone less drunk than the miller would surely have detected the fraud; but there were no other witnesses, and the cheat went undetected. The trick was turned, and the honest miller lost his great treasure.

After Christopher Midgett had staggered, sobbing,

from the game room of the Toney House, the winner settled back to gloat privately over his winnings and to count his money. It was then long past midnight, and the single candle on the table before him gave out a feeble, flickering light as the trickster finished off the bottle and once again examined the ring he had won.

"Magic, bah!" snorted the pack peddler, as he contemptuously rubbed hard with the ball of his right thumb against the surface of the great pearl. The ring itself immediately vanished in a huge flash of phosphorescent light which filled the game room. There, bathed in the eerie light of the sea, towered Poseidon himself, trident held tightly in his muscular right fist and a terrible anger flashing from his sea-green eyes.

"Speak, mortal!" he roared in a voice like the awful winds of a hurricane. "You have gained my ring and the miller's third wish by trickery, but the King of the Sea keeps his word, and that wish is now yours. The wish! What is the wish? Speak it now or lose it forever."

The startled peddler had fallen over backwards onto the floor at the sudden apparition. Now he scrambled to his knees, and folding his hands together in a gesture of supplication, he tried to bring order to his wildly confused thoughts. So the ring had been magic all along! Here was the King of the Sea offering him anything in the world he wanted. All the riches of all the kingdoms in the world could be his, along with all the power and admiration those riches would surely bring.

It is indicative of the character of the man that, in this time of unexpected crisis and possible danger, his first thought was still to enrich himself, to make a profit.

Crafty as ever, he feared that a misstep now might bring awful vengeance down upon him in the form of the razor-sharp prongs of that threatening trident. So, seeking as always to be devious, he decided not to wish for all the treasure in the world as was his first inclination. He would make a sly wish that, unknown to this Poseidon, would very soon make him the world's richest man. His thoughts flew to the money pouch in his upstairs room. He had often been fascinated by the manner in which arithmetical figures, when doubled and redoubled several times, would soon climb to astronomical heights. In his drunken state, he immediately seized on this as his solution, and his scheming heart leaped with joy and anticipation.

"Master," he quavered from his kneeling position, "it is my wish that the contents of my leather pouch should double and redouble every hour, on the hour."

"Which leather pouch?" roared Poseidon in a voice that made the very rafters ring and echo.

And there the pack peddler was undone. He could not remember which pouch held what at the moment. He frantically cudgeled his brain to come up with the right answer. The greedy sharper was at last caught in the oldest of sucker games, the old shell game, and he had trapped himself. For the life of him, he couldn't tell which shell contained the pea or, rather, which pouch contained the cash.

"Which one?" howled Poseidon again. "Tell me, and tell me now, or I'll gig you with my trident as you deserve."

In desperation the peddler made his guess. "The black leather pouch, sire. The black one. Yes, I am sure that is the right one. It is the black leather pouch I speak of."

"Granted," intoned Poseidon in a voice that was newly calm and peaceful. "Your wish is now granted and the ring has returned to my treasury in the sea." With these words, the majestic King of the Sea gradually faded away. He grew dimmer and dimmer, until only the razor-sharp points of his royal trident twinkled like bright stars in the darkness. As these glimmered out, the candle on the table also went out, and complete darkness filled the room along with a lingering smell of phosphorous.

Bursting with eagerness and curiosity, the peddler sprang from the floor, now practically cold sober. Bumping against the table and chairs in the darkness, he stumbled out of the room and up the stairs to his own quarters. It seemed to him as though it took him forever to light a candle with his trembling hands. Finally, with the lighted candle, he approached his back pack lying there on the bed.

A broad smile creased his face as he heard a new sound, a sharp clicking noise emanating from his pack. Pulling open the large sack, he dug hastily through its contents, throwing the green leather pouch over his shoulder and scattering fishhooks over the room, and flinging the white leather pouch against the wall and dumping needles on the floor. In his eagerness to get to that clicking black leather bag, he slammed the brown leather pouch against the head of his bed, and instantly his body froze in disbelief. Out of the loosened mouth of the brown pouch trickled the cash money he had so carefully hidden there. He had guessed wrong. The money had been in the brown sack all along.

In a frenzy of rage, the peddler snatched up the clicking black bag and confirmed his suspicions. There, in that black pouch already nearly bursting at the seams with its steadily increasing contents, was nothing but straight pins! Already, there were thousands of straight pins, all shiny and bright and sharp-pointed. Already, their number was doubling and redoubling every hour as they spilled off the bed and onto the floor.

Running to the open window, the pack peddler threw the black leather bag and all its contents just as far as he could hurl it in the direction of a little sand hill outside the window. Suddenly, there was a strong gust of wind blowing directly toward that little dune and a sound like muffled, gargantuan laughter, which rolled on and on and finally diminished like thunder in a summer sky. The multiplying pins scattered all over the crest of that little hill, and the pouch began to be covered by the drifting sands.

Well, that is the story of Pin Hill. The very old man who told the story, and who certainly ought to know, says his parents often stayed in the Toncy House before it was finally engulfed by drifting sand.

It is said that the black leather bag is still doubling and redoubling its contents every hour on the hour under the sands of Pin Hill. It is also said that, if all the pins on the surface of the hill were gathered together, there would be an ample supply spread all over the place by the next morning. Some of the pins are rusted together as though they have been there for a very long time. Others are fused into sheafs from four to six inches long. And they are there right now, even as your eyes read these lines.

White Stallion

Mustee is an American word that is not used much any more, but it was heard often in colonial and pre-colonial days in coastal North Carolina, particularly on the Outer Banks.

Long before the Sir Walter Raleigh colonists came to these shores, Giovanni da Verrazzano's exploring ship visited Hatteras and other points on these islands to obtain fresh meat and water. According to folk memory, they got fresh water and deer meat, but they suffered the loss of three crewmen who disappeared into the woods with friendly natives, never to return to the ship. These seamen are said to have married into the resident Indian tribes, and their offspring became known as mustees. Not half-breeds. Mustees. You see, the name is said to have come down from an even more ancient intermingling of foreign blood. And thereby hangs our tale.

Go back with me now in history to the sixty-fourth year after the birth of our Lord, Jesus, the Christus. The insane Nero ruled in Rome, and Rome was the absolute master of the known world. The Romans, at that time, were skilled shipbuilders and master mariners. Supporting their occupation forces in Gaul and Britain required stout supply ships, and these they had. The military and merchant forces were in possession of large, worthy vessels such as Saint Paul told of when he recounted his voyage on a Roman ship capable of carrying three hundred passengers in addition to her crew. Because the Roman sailors had to contend with the sudden, angry mistrals, which sometimes blow up unexpectedly to scourge the waters of the Mediterranean, they had to be brave as well as cautious (an admirable combination of traits for sailors of any day), and their sailing ships, as well as their galleys, had to be well-found. Most of their sailing techniques had been learned from the conquered Egyptians, but the Romans had learned their lessons well.

THE FLAMING SHIP OF OCRACOKE

Old, mad Nero was in full spree. He had already crowned his beautiful, white Arabian stallion as ruler of Rome and had gone the full list of orgies. He had long since murdered his mother and his wife, but his own suicide was still four years in the future. Now, he had two pet projects. The first was what must have been one of the earlier urban renewal projects in history—the burning of the entire city of Rome. The second was the scientific killing of the members of the Christian religion by every means his depraved mind could contrive.

According to tradition, some sixty or seventy of the yet undiscovered Roman Christians were working as stevedores and dock workers in the port of Rome some distance from the city. They were unloading a large grain ship which lay moored to the wharf, and they talked quietly among themselves of the worsening conditions. They could see the black billows of smoke rising from the city, and they knew well that hundreds of their Christian brothers were dying in those flames every day.

Early that evening word came that a detachment of Nero's soldiers was on its way to arrest them. The exhausted messenger warned that they were to be seized just before first light and hauled back into the city to face a mock trial before the Emperor—then death.

In those perilous days, a Christian stayed alive only if he gave credence to such rumors and took prompt action, and that is exactly what tradition says those Roman Christians did. They overpowered the unarmed grain ship crew and took the ship. They filled every cask and barrel with fresh water and stowed such food aboard as they could find. Before dawn, those dock workers, accompanied by their wives and children, cast off the ship's moorings and set sail westward toward the Pillars of Hercules, as the Strait of Gibraltar was then called. Some of the Christians were excellent sailors themselves, and many of the overpowered crew members joined them gladly in their dash for freedom.

It is told that a sudden storm blew them quickly westward very soon after they cast off, and, by dawn's first light, they were already out of sight of the Italian mainland. Tradition says that they were pursued far out into the Atlantic Ocean. It was accepted in those days that, if you sailed far enough westward in the Atlantic Ocean, you would sail right off the edge of the earth and fall through space for all eternity, so the pursuers finally lost their nerve and turned back. To those desperate Christians, however, it could have made but little difference. Falling off the edge of the earth was still not so bad as being torn to pieces by wild beasts in Nero's games or being tossed, still living, upon the giant funeral pyre that was Rome. For them there could be no turning back—not ever!

With a ship half-filled with grain and with plenty of drinking water, they had a fighting chance. The winds were favorable easterlies, and rain came from time to time to help replenish their water supply. It was a different kind of wilderness, that desert of salt water, but they had faith in their God and confidence that He would see them through. It seems certain that many of them died and were buried at sea, but it is almost equally certain that some of them did manage to survive. Here is where history and tradition draw the curtain of the centuries, and we must turn to legend to continue the story.

When the first English explorers landed on the Outer Banks, they ran into recurrent accounts of an already ancient legend. From Corolla to Core Banks, the folk memory was always the same. Many generations ago some people had come in a great boat with wings and had landed or wrecked on those shores. Some of those light-skinned people had settled with the tribes on the Banks; others had pushed further westward up the mighty river the Indians called Roanoke, moving from tribe to tribe and always being made welcome. Folk memory has it that they found a place of happy and permanent settlement far up the river, though they eventually died out as a separate race or were absorbed through intermarriage. The ones on the Outer Banks also intermarried with the friendly coastal Indians, and their offspring, from the very first, were known as mustees—a very special kind of people.

Until centuries later, when the white man ran the Indians off those coastal islands and took them over for his own, a curious admixture of Indian nature worship and what seemed to be a type of Christianity persisted among those people. Many symbols that, for centuries, had been associated with Christianity, such as the cross and the fish, existed in the very same culture with the Indian swastika and picture language.

By and large, the first mustees were said to have been beautiful and intelligent people, but with the coming of many more shipwreck survivors in the fifteen hundreds and their subsequent marriages with both Indians and mustees, the racial lines became much more mixed. In time, the word mustee came to mean, not necessarily a good or fine person, but simply one who had both Indian and white blood mixed in his veins.

Around Corolla, however, the pure crossing of the Indian with the Italian was preserved. The result was a community or subtribe of outstanding beauty, strength, and intelligence, which professed and adhered to many practices and principles that seemed to be of Christian origin. By tribal custom, each of the chiefs was named White Stallion, with no attempt at numbering. Upon being made chief, a warrior immediately adopted the title and wore it until his death.

In the time with which this story deals, the last of the Indians and mustees had not yet been run off the Banks by the encroaching white man. Around Corolla, they still lived in peace and plenty. The settlers had "granted" them fishing and grazing rights, and they clung to their ancient ways. The current Chief White Stallion was an impressive figure of a man, standing well over six feet tall. He had a proud, erect carriage and a dignified mien. A lifetime of active, outdoor living had given him the musculature of a trained athlete and tremendous physical strength. But, with all his physical prowess, he was a remarkably gentle man. The strange blending of Christian-like ideals with tribal taboos had made him long-suffering and slow to anger. Only when he was convinced that he had been knowingly wronged did his temper show. On these rare occasions, his anger was said to be awful to behold. He was then just as savage as he was usually mild, as bent on revenge as he had been long-suffering.

THE FLAMING SHIP OF OCRACOKE

It is remembered that his daughter, White Fawn, was every bit as lovely as her father was handsome. She was the only child of his now deceased mustee bride, and White Stallion loved her with a fierce, proud affection. She was the brightest spot in his entire life, and their dwelling was a happy one. White Fawn was of medium height with eyes of startling blueness and fine, regular features. She would have caused heads to turn and eyes to gleam in any civilization.

It was her beauty of spirit, though, that made her the darling of the entire tribe. Always kind and generous, she was sincerely interested in the well-being of each of her people. She was never too tired or too busy to counsel them on their problems, to weep with them in their grief, or to rejoice with them in their happiness. She possessed that priceless faculty of making everyone feel important and meaningful. No wonder whites, Indians, and mustees all loved and respected her.

No wonder, either, that Benjamin Smith fell head over heels in love with her. He was a sturdy young Englishman, fresh from the British Isles, who had immigrated to this new land and had bargained to buy and pay for a large farm on Currituck Banks. He had never seen such a woman as White Fawn. The young Briton was of an impetuous nature and attractive in his own way because of his adventurous spirit and devil-may-care, merry disposition. That he soon tired of each new undertaking he attempted was generally overlooked by his friends because of the enthusiasm with which he attacked new projects. Nothing held his interest for very long, but while that interest lasted, he was indefatigable in the pursuit of his goals.

So, young Benjamin Smith rushed White Fawn off her feet with his ardent courtship. The mustee princess responded to the whirlwind romance with all the love in her naive, gentle heart; soon she shyly confessed to her father that she wanted Smith for her husband. The suitor and White Stallion met in formal council, and Benjamin asked for White Fawn's hand in marriage, promising to build her a fine home there on Currituck Banks, where she could still be close to her father and yet run the home of the prosperous young farmer Smith intended to be. The Chief gave his consent, and the couple became engaged.

Construction began immediately on the frame house in Currituck Woods just north of the present site of Corolla and near Penny Hill. The foundations were laid in short order, but after that, the construction moved slowly. It was one of the busy fishing seasons, and most of the able-bodied men who had been working on the house were out tending their nets. It was essential that they lay in as large a supply of fish as possible for salting down against the winter, when fishing would not be reliable enough to guarantee food for their households.

During this time, trouble for White Fawn appeared on the scene in the form of a beautiful young Irish girl, who had lost both parents and had come to live with a wealthy uncle at Currituck. She brought with her, so it was said, a considerable cash dowry for the man who should be lucky enough to make her his bride.

Well, that was the way it happened. The more Smith thought of the pretty colleen and her dowry, the better she looked to him and the more he had second thoughts about his engagement to White Fawn. Finally, the uncle asked Benjamin exactly what his intentions were in seeing so much of his orphaned niece when it was well known that he was engaged to the mustee princess, White Fawn. That put it squarely to Smith, and in his usual impetuous manner, he decided then and there that it was the Irish girl and her dowry he wanted and not the beautiful mustee. He told the uncle of his desire to make the young woman his wife, and it was agreed that he would be accepted as a suitor, but only after he had broken with White Fawn.

Of course, White Fawn knew nothing about this turn of events, and she was completely crushed when Benjamin broke off their engagement. She just could not believe it, though she immediately released Smith from his promise and wished him well. From that day on, she went into a physical decline that ended in her death less than a year later. It was as if she had lost all interest in living and had willed herself to die.

Benjamin Smith was man enough to seek out White Stallion after he had told White Fawn the bad news. The meeting took place in White Stallion's thatched dwelling, and strict Indian taboo forbade the injury of any guest in the Chief's home. This is what probably saved Smith's life, because the father's anger was terrible to behold. Seizing his heavy hunting spear in his brawny right fist, he towered above Benjamin Smith, every muscle in his body quivering with rage. Instant murder flashed in his eyes, and for a few long minutes, the Englishman's life hung in delicate balance.

Legend says that he did not kill the faithless suitor, however. By the time the meeting ended, reason had returned to the Chief's mind, and he resolutely put behind him the great temptation to skewer this false suitor like a gigged flounder. Instead, he called down an awful curse on Smith and all his descendants and their friends. With many incantations and prayers to spirits, White Stallion pronounced his curse: that the house near Penny Hill, which was begun for White Fawn, should forever be haunted because of the wrong done to her, to the extent that no one should ever be able to live there.

And the remarkable thing about it is, no one has.

Mr. George Scarborough, uncle of the present postmaster at Nag's Head, knows. He tells about the time, long past, when he was offered the house rent-free just to stay there and keep things in shape. He moved there during the dark of the moon, and one of the first things he did was to plant a large garden plot beside the house. On the first moonlit night, he says, he was nearly scared out of his wits when he looked out a window and beheld a huge white stallion rearing and kicking in rage, and all the while giving out the most hideous screams and whistles imaginable. All about the raging horse a sort of eerie glow appeared, as though he were illuminated by some light from within. Bloodstained foam flecked his nostrils, and his eyes gleamed with a fire quite unlike anything Mr. Scarborough had ever seen before. The good man was sure that his newly planted garden was ruined, but he wasn't about to go out into that moonlit night to investigate. The next morning he found not a hill, nor a furrow, not a row of his garden disturbed. The very spot where that stallion had pawed the earth in his fury was as smooth and unmarked as it had been when Scarborough finished with it.

George Scarborough, brave man that he was, stuck it out for a few more days, but he says that his nerves just couldn't stand it. A man has to have some sleep in order to keep his sanity, and sleep with that ghost stallion raging about was impossible. Rent-free or not, the house was simply not worth it to George Scarborough, and he sadly moved away and has not spent a night there since.

And that is where the matter stands. That fine, old house, built by Smith at great expense, is still standing near Penny Hill a little north of Corolla, but, to this day, no one, Smith or non-Smith, has ever been able to stand living there.

If you do not believe in ghosts or curses, if you insist that there is a logical explanation for everything that happens, and if you have the nerve, maybe you can arrange to spend a night at the house of the white stallion. It should be easy enough to determine who the present owners are and to ask their permission to spend a night (or part of a night) there, when the moon casts its white beams over Penny Hill and you are miles away from any other human and the winds begin to whine and whistle over the dunes.

Just don't say that you weren't warned.

Sea-born Woman

The year was 1720, and the month was the often stormy September. The Irish emigrant ship, *Celestial Harp*, had made heavy weather of the voyage since leaving Belfast several weeks before. Head winds and stormy seas had made the trip a succession of miserable days and rest-broken nights for the poor emigrants huddled below decks. The stench from the whale-oil lamps swinging from the low ceiling mixed with the human odors inevitable in such close confinement. The sickening roll and pitch of the ship distressed many an already queasy stomach, and the pitiful passengers were a sorry-looking lot indeed.

Most of them had worked long and hard, had scrimped and saved to accumulate passage money for this trip. Conditions were almost intolerably hard for the poor in Ireland at that time, and the dream of a life in that New World across the sea seemed, to many, like the hope of a Promised Land, a land of opportunity and of beginning again. This was the dream that sustained them. This was the vision that, even now, was stronger than the fear of sudden shipwreck and death in the stormy North Atlantic.

John and Mary O'Hagan considered themselves to be more fortunate than most of the emigrants. John had his skill in carpentry, which was sure to be much in demand in the new country, and Mary had the frugality and good common sense of the typical Irish housewife. More than that, Mary was expecting the birth of their first child any day now, and, thank God, there were two midwives in the company, thus assuring her the very best of care. The O'Hagans considered themselves to be greatly blessed.

Two days earlier the weather had cleared, and, as if an omen of brighter days to come, the wind had abated and hauled favorably and the seas had subsided. At long last, the emigrants were able to come out on deck and enjoy the sights, sounds, and fresh smells of a brisk day at sea. Their joy was complete when the Captain told them that the worst weather was now past and that they were almost within sight of Massachusetts Colony, where they could expect to land within the week.

Just over the horizon, some twenty or thirty miles to the southward, another group of seafarers was also rejoicing over the improvement in the weather. The flotilla of five pirate ships under the command of the famous buccaneer captain, Edward Low, had had very poor hunting, and the motley crews were eager and fretting for action. Discipline had become more of a problem than ever among the cutthroat sailors, and there had even been rumblings of a possible mutiny and a departure to warmer climes and better hunting grounds.

The pirates had come north hoping to intercept merchant ships loaded with valuable cargoes but, so far, had encountered only the huge, crashing, green seas of the North Atlantic. The gale-force winds had blown almost incessantly, and never a potential quarry had come into view, although many could have slipped past undetected in the driving rain and mist. The sudden break in the weather and the reappearance of the sun brightened the spirits of the sea rovers, and they were literally spoiling for action.

This mission had been undertaken jointly by the five ships, so when the weather improved, Captain Low called a hurried conference of his captains on the afterdeck of his ship. There it was decided that three of the five vessels would sail in various southerly directions in search of prey. Low's ship and the *Delight*, captained by Low's favorite subordinate, Francis Carrington Spriggs, would sail in still other directions towards the north. Rendezvous was set for six months later at New Providence, which at that time served as one of the major pirate capitals of the world.

Just before first light the next morning, Spriggs and his crew of eighteen weighed anchor on the *Delight*, eased the ship away from Low's ship, and made full sail northward in the darkness. As the *Delight* squared away on her new course and left the other ships behind, Captain Spriggs himself raised his new flag swiftly to the main truck, the highest point on the vessel. The crew cheered lustily at the sight of this sinister symbol of piracy, and several broke into a clumsy sort of hornpipe dance. The young captain had designed the flag to suit his own particular taste, and it was unique in the pirate world. It consisted of a large rectangular piece of black cloth on which was sewn the figure of a white skeleton holding an hourglass in one bony hand and an arrow on which was impaled a bleeding heart in the other hand. The flag snapped in the fresh, early morning breeze as though it had a life of its own.

Northward then drove the *Delight* and her newly independent captain. A fresh breeze poured over her port quarter, and her damp sails were set and drawing well. Northward she sped and, as fate would have it, on a course which would intercept that of the plodding *Celestial Harp* and her human cargo.

It was about first light the next morning when the lookout in the main shrouds of the pirate ship cried his sighting of the emigrant vessel. By midday the two ships lay alongside each other and the brief resistance on the part of the crew of the *Celestial Harp* had ended. The shipload of pitiful passengers were now all pirate captives and in very real danger of immediate and violent death.

Captain Spriggs' disappointment at the poverty of his prize can be imagined. The captured ship, herself, was too slow and clumsy to be worth confiscating, and the few supplies she had left were hardly worth transferring to his own craft. The anger of the pirate skipper was an evil token for his captives. Even for one so young, Captain Spriggs was already building a reputation, not only for bravery, but for cruelty, for it was his habit to put to death all captured seamen so that they might not later testify against him. "Dead men tell no tales," he had cried on more than one occasion such as this, and he was prepared to practice his philosophy now.

Maybe it was because of his disappointment or maybe it was just to impress his crew that he now devised a new and more dramatic way to close forever the mouths of his captives. Pirate crews were always notoriously close to mutiny, and an example of savagery was usually helpful in keeping them in their place. Whatever the reason, the method of extermination, this time, was to be most unusual.

Personally supervising his crew, Spriggs ordered kegs of gunpowder secured at strategic places near the water-line of the emigrant ship. Fuses of varying lengths were then run from these powder kegs to a central spot on the deck. According to the pirate's calculations, if he lighted the fuses at one-minute intervals, he would have time to get off the doomed ship and, then, all the powder kegs would explode simultaneously, blowing the ship to bits. The men of the *Celestial Harp*, passengers and crew alike, were chained to masts and stanchions so that they could neither interfere with the grand explosion nor leap into the sea to save themselves. The careful planning and preparation was all accomplished before the terrified eyes of the chained men, whose pleading and prayers the pirates scornfully ignored. This was to be a blast that would live in pirate history.

Meanwhile, below the foredeck and completely unknown to the pirates, another drama was taking place. The two midwives, working in frantic haste, were preparing for the birth of Mary O'Hagan's child. Whether or not the excitement and despair caused by the pirate invasion had hastened the event, there was now no time to consider, nor did it matter. The greatest of God's recurring miracles was about to take place, and the three women most immediately concerned would not be bothered with what was going on above decks, even though death itself might be imminent. A baby was about to be born.

Thus was Mary O'Hagan delivered of a beautiful, large baby girl in the dim light of swinging oil lamps in the stuffy hold of a ship which was hove to and rolling restlessly in the waves. A delighted smile creased the face of the elder midwife as she held the new-born child up by the ankles and slapped her smartly with an open hand across the little buttocks. The sound of the first healthy wail from the baby's lungs echoed and reechoed in the confines of the hold, penetrated the hatch openings, and sounded on the deck of the *Celestial Harp*, where men stood ready to torture and kill upon their leader's signal.

What prompted Captain Francis Spriggs' next move is known only to God. It could have been that he felt some stirring of pity for his helpless victims after his first anger at their poverty had passed. It could have been that he suddenly remembered an ancient superstition of pirates that it is very lucky for a new captain to release his first prize, just as some fishermen always throw back the first fish caught. It is quite possible that he quickly realized that the blessed event provided him with a means of saving face before his crew, while making his offering on the altar of luck at the same time. Whatever the reason, he reacted immediately.

Beaming with honest joy when he was told of the birth, he sent below to inquire if the new-born baby was a boy or a girl. Upon learning that the child was a girl, he fairly capered with delight. He pointed again and again, first to the name board of his own ship where the title *Delight* appeared in foot-high gilt letters, then back to the hatchway from whence came the lusty cries of the baby. He seemed to sense some connection between the ship's name and the arrival of the child, and the coincidence pleased him beyond measure.

Summoning the master of the emigrant ship, the first mate, and the baby's father John O'Hagan, the pirate chieftain made them a proposition. "Only name the baby girl for my dear old mother," he said, "and I'll let your ship go free. Call her Jerushia—Jerushia Spriggs O'Hagan —and you can all go with my blessing."

Well, it didn't take them long to accept such a one-sided choice as that, and so the bargain was made. The gunpowder kegs and unlit fuses were removed from the

Celestial Harp as the baby's name was entered in the ship's log as Jerushia Spriggs O'Hagan. Both John and Mary O'Hagan signed the book in agreement to the name, and it was duly witnessed by both midwives, the Captain, and the first mate.

So pleased was Captain Spriggs with the acceptance of his offer that he immediately sent a small boat back to the *Delight* to fetch a bolt of cloth-of-gold, which he gave to Mary O'Hagan with the strict admonition that it be used only to make a wedding gown for Jerushia when she was grown to womanhood and had chosen her man.

On this note, the two ships parted. The *Celestial Harp* plowed, once again, on her way to Massachusetts, and the *Delight* headed southward, her cannon booming out a long, rolling salute of twelve guns as the distance widened between the vessels.

In the New World, John O'Hagan's skills with the drawing knife, the saw, and the chisel stood him in good stead. Settling in New Bedford, he developed into one of the finest shipbuilders available, and his services were much in demand. As he worked and prospered, little Jerushia grew and developed until the fame of her Irish beauty spread far and wide. The sea baby had become beautiful on a majestic scale. A full six feet tall she was, slender and graceful. To set off her willowy figure, she was blessed with hair the color of mahogany, which fell like a cape to her waist. With lovely, regular features and an open, sunny disposition, she was the favorite of young and old. Only one incident marred those golden years. When she was twelve, Jerushia's mother died, and the duties of the household fell on her young shoulders.

All during those happy years, there was never a Christmas which passed without a very special gift from Captain Spriggs, and, on each birthday, he sent her a bolt of very fine cloth of some description from which she delighted in making her own special dresses. The pirate had searched out the whereabouts of the girl he had spared and took pleasure in remembering her special days. Jerushia called him "Godfather," although she actually saw him only a very few times during those years.

In due time, she chose from among her many suitors a young sea captain. She was married in New Bedford, in a dress of Captain Spriggs' cloth-of-gold. The union was blessed with three children, all boys. It was, indeed, a happy period in Jerushia's life, a time of loving and sharing, of growth and blessed contentment.

What happened to Captain Francis Spriggs for several years after that September day in 1720, when he sailed away from the reprieved *Celestial Harp*, is not clear. It is almost certain that he did sail back to the pirate rendezvous at New Providence, for if he had not, his fellow pirates would have hunted him down and murdered him for breaking faith with the Brotherhood of the Sea, as they called themselves. Apparently, his career as a pirate did not last very long, however. According to British Navy records, he met his first, and only, defeat fairly soon after the *Celestial Harp* incident. While plundering the Bay of Honduras, Spriggs and his crew were surprised by a British warship. The *Delight* was run aground, and Spriggs and his ruffians escaped to shore.

There are no more official accounts of his pirating and, so far as the records of the British Admiralty show, he just dropped out of sight. There is no evidence that he ever took the King's Pardon, as so many of the Brotherhood who wanted to come ashore and live as honest men did. Neither is there any record that he thereafter engaged in any unlawful activity. His faithful remembering of Jerushia's birthdays and Christmases provides the only record of him at all for many years.

But, in 1741, Spriggs again surfaced on the sea of history as we catch a glimpse of him in Yorktown, Virginia. Here he was a ship owner and merchant of considerable means, owning several vessels engaged in trade with foreign countries. There is a record of his business and an account of his marriage and of the death of his bride in less than a year in one of the terrible epidemics of those times. Still later it is known that he moved to Beaufort Town, sometimes called Hongry Town in that era, for a few years.

Meanwhile, the shadow of tragedy had fallen on Jerushia. Her father was killed in a shipyard accident, and, in a terrible storm in 1758, her husband and her youngest son were lost at sea. Her oldest son had become a preacher and went to live as a missionary among the Indians of the western plains. Her second son took over a portion of his father's business, but he married a woman as different from his mother as can be imagined. There always seemed to be some difference, some misunderstanding, between the two women, and Jerushia, while adequately provided for, lived a very lonely life. There was not much a widow could do in New Bedford in those days and, to make things worse, the business began to suffer reverses. Soon Jerushia was reduced to very modest circumstances and, at times, she felt the pinch of actual want.

This was the atmosphere when, in September of that year, her birthday came around and, for the very first time, no delivery van brought the customary bolt of cloth to her door. Already depressed, she broke down and cried miserably. Later that afternoon, she answered the bell at her door and saw, standing before her, a figure that was at once familiar and yet unfamiliar.

Her caller was a tall, erect man in his early sixties with graying hair and deeply tanned, but young-looking, skin. Some little thing, some mannerism of his as he removed his hat with a flourish and smiled at her, served to trigger her memory. With a rush of happiness, she recognized "Godfather Spriggs" and, like a little girl, threw her arms around his neck in welcome.

What a time those two must have had reminiscing on that day! The bolt of cloth was not missing; Francis Spriggs had brought it with him. He was in New Bedford on business, he told her, and must leave within the week. She told him of her loneliness, and he called on the young woman daily while he was there, telling her of his plans and his problems.

Having accumulated a great deal of wealth, he planned to retire from the world of business, for he wanted nothing more from life than to spend his remaining years somewhere near the sea, where he could read and perhaps tend a little garden and listen to the talk of seafaring men. He had purchased a plot of ground in a North Carolina town called Portsmouth, which was just south of Ocracoke Inlet and just across that inlet from Pilot Town, as some people called the village of Ocracoke. The Colony of Carolina was developing this town, and it was to be the biggest seaport anywhere around, with wharves and warehouses and shipfitting basins. There were many stores and shops and even plans for a large hospital to be located there. He had bought his plot at a reasonable price from his old friend, Colonel Michael Coutanch of Bath Town, and was even now building a two-story house with all the most modern conveniences known to the building trade.

Knowing Jerushia's loneliness, he asked her to move to Portsmouth as his housekeeper. In return, he offered her an excellent salary, considerate treatment, and the promise of the house itself at his death. Jerushia accepted the offer gladly, and thus began another of the happiest periods of her life.

Housekeeper she was, indeed, but Captain Spriggs, from the very first, treated her more like a daughter than a servant. Old enough to be her father and without children of his own, he lavished on her all the comforts he would have given to his own children. Jerushia had to plan the meals and buy provisions in the village of Portsmouth, but Spriggs provided her with a cook and a maid to do the heavy cleaning. Knowing her love of horses, he bought her a matched pair of black Arabians and a shiny black buggy to ride in. What a beautiful sight it must have been to see this tall, lovely woman, dressed all in widow's black but with a wealth of dark red hair streaming out behind her, as she drove her horses at full speed down the one road that extended the length of Portsmouth Island or walked them into Portsmouth Town to shop for groceries!

As Captain Spriggs had promised, "Spriggs' Luck," as

the house was called, had all the conveniences known in that day. The ground floor was comprised of a large parlor and an equally large dining room. Off to one side was a sitting room and, on the other, a combination library-office, where the Captain handled the details of the shipping business in which he was still engaged. It was here that he also entertained his infrequent business visitors.

The second story contained four large bedrooms, and, out back, a dogtrot (now called a breezeway) connected the house with the kitchen and pantry, which were built separate from the main structure in order to protect the main house from the hazard of fire and the odors of cooking. The "necessary house" was a rather commodious two-room structure built some fifty or sixty feet to the rear of the kitchen and reached via a roofed, brick walkway extending from the back door of the kitchen. Thus it was entirely possible to walk, during a pouring rainstorm, from the main house through the dogtrot and the kitchen to the necessary house without once feeling a drop of rain or setting foot on the bare ground.

Spriggs' Luck had one macabre feature. In the large parlor there was a huge fireplace, complete with andirons and an iron cooking hook. The hearthstone in front of this opening was a large slab of solid marble some six inches thick, which served also as the lid for a concrete burial vault located immediately underneath. It was Spriggs' fancy that he wanted to be buried here so that his body would always be above the reach of the storm tides and still be part and parcel of the house that he loved so well. He had seen what those storms could, and sometimes would, do to an ordinary graveyard, and the thought haunted him. He made Jerushia promise that, should she outlive him, she would see that his burial was exactly as he wanted it.

Located well to the rear of the building was a small peach orchard with fifteen or twenty peach trees and a small pergola, or summerhouse, nestled in the center. Here the housekeeper could while away the afternoon hours of a spring day at reading or making lace, with the scent of the many bay trees and the peach blossoms heavy in the air and the muted sound of the surf in the middle distance. Off to one side were the carriage house and the stables where her blooded horses were kept.

Jerushia was far from selfish in her happiness. As though sensing in some way that she could not keep good fortune unless she shared it with those less happy, she became a veritable angel of mercy to the womenfolk of Portsmouth Town and Portsmouth Island. She trained herself to become as skillful as any midwife at the many duties surrounding childbirth, and her warm sympathy and ready wit made her a welcome assistant in times of stress and trouble. On her frequent trips by boat to New Berne and Beaufort and Edenton, she always inquired ahead of time what her neighbors would like brought to them. If she had to add a coin or two from her own purse to make up an unexpectedly high purchase price, no one was ever the wiser.

The unusual circumstances surrounding her birth soon became known to the island women, and, with the mysticism that comes so naturally to coastland folk, she became known simply as Sea-born Woman. As time passed, the people of Portsmouth grew to love her and rely on her and trust her.

So far as Jerushia knew, her benefactor did not have an enemy in the world. The days of his piratical beginnings were long past and almost never mentioned. The days flowed by like a lazy stream, and Captain Spriggs seemed happy to live in Spriggs' Luck, taking part in an occasional fishing of the gill nets with friends from the village or conferring with an occasional visitor about some business matter. There were long, sunlit days in summer, too, when the Captain and his housekeeper would stroll the ocean beach of Portsmouth Island for miles. They would watch the many ships that used the port and wonder whence they came and whither they were bound.

Enemies he must have had, however, and they eventually searched him out and found him. Returning from the village late one afternoon in the winter of 1770, Jerushia wheeled her horses into the wide circle she usually described before entering the stables. As she approached the stable yard, both horses reared and shied in fright, so that it required all her strength to control them. In the fading light of the setting sun she saw, to her horror, what had frightened them. There on the sand lay Captain Spriggs, face down, with a dirk driven to the hilt between his shoulder blades. He was quite dead.

The footprints that must have marked the sandy soil had all been carefully erased with a branch broken from one of the peach trees. Near the body lay half of a sheet of parchment, and, in the center of that parchment, a black spot about the size of a shilling had been laboriously inscribed with a quill and black ink. The pirate mark of revenge-death!

All efforts to find the killer or killers proved futile. There were no strangers in town other than the usual polyglot assortment of sailors on leave from the many ships that lay at anchor in the harbor. There was no way to or from the island except by boat; nevertheless, it was impossible to find even one logical suspect.

As the old pirate had wished, Sea-born Woman buried him in the vault he had prepared. Sailors and local fishermen rigged a block and tackle to hoist the marble hearthstone so that the body could be lowered into the vault. Then the marble was cemented back into place to make an airtight seal. And, true to his word, Spriggs had left a will in his own handwriting, bequeathing Spriggs' Luck and all the surrounding grounds to Jerushia.

From that moment on, Jerushia lived not only in that house, but largely for that house. Always a good housekeeper, she now made a fetish of keeping Spriggs' Luck in immaculate condition. Never a speck of dust was allowed to accumulate on the fine furniture. In the spring and summer, she placed fresh flowers in the fireplace opening just alongside the marble hearthstone. Often passersby at night would see her lonely figure seated in a chair in front of that hearth, a whale-oil lamp burning brightly on a table by her side.

When the American Revolution flared into full hostilities, Ocracoke Inlet and Portsmouth Harbor became two of the focal points of combat. The deep-water channel through Ocracoke Inlet was then, as it is now, a twisting, hazardous, and ever-changing thing. Raiding

British warships had to be of shallow draft to negotiate that channel, and, once inside the bar, they found American galleys, manned by patriots at the long oar sweeps, awaiting them. Resembling ancient Roman slave galleys, these oar-driven vessels were very swift and maneuverable and were usually more than a match for the slower Britishers. Thus, Portsmouth and Ocracoke harbors, as well as the Town of Portsmouth, often rang with the sound of naval gunfire, as miniature naval engagements were fought to the death in those sheltered waters.

Raiding parties of British Marines were often put ashore to forage and to burn the countryside and kill all the livestock they could find. These invading forces were met by small groups of militia formed by the native fishermen. Usually the advantage lay with the islanders. They knew the terrain and were perfectly at home in that environment of sand and wind and roaring surf. The British had the better weapons, though, and the advantage of professional training as soldiers with the discipline of regulars. In spite of this, no actual occupation of Portsmouth Town was ever achieved by the British, although they kept considerable pressure on the thin defensive forces stationed there.

For the five or six years the fighting actually lasted on the Outer Banks, Jerushia was a tower of strength to her people. She converted Spriggs' Luck into a very efficient hospital and recruited and trained several of the local ladies as nurses. Reading avidly such medical books as she could find, she did her best to relieve, mend, and cure the casualties brought to her beloved home. The islanders had always been fond of her. Now they began to regard her as a special saint who had been sent especially for their healing and comfort. They tipped their hats or pulled at their forelocks in gestures of respect and admiration when the tall, graceful figure, dressed always in black, walked by. They relied on her, and she never failed them as long as she lived. She was the living spirit of Portsmouth Town for many, many years, and she helped them to persevere until the Revolution was won.

Sea-born Woman died in her sleep one peaceful spring night in 1810 at the ripe old age of ninety. She was tenderly and lovingly laid to rest in the little yaupon grove to the rear of Spriggs' Luck by her friends and neighbors. There had been no illness, no suffering, no long period of disability. It is said that she just stopped living very quietly and easily.

But if the natives thought that they had seen the last of this remarkable woman when they buried her, they were mistaken. Some three years later the first recorded appearance of what is said to be her ghost took place.

During the War of 1812, when the British came so close to retaking their former American colonies, the first manifestation occurred. In 1813, the King's forces landed on Portsmouth Island and began the systematic slaughter of all the livestock they could find in order, they claimed, to procure fresh meat for their ships lying offshore. Houses were ransacked and looted, and many islanders were robbed of their few valuable possessions. It was inevitable that a fine structure like Spriggs' Luck, now boarded up and tightly shuttered, should be the object of such an attack.

An English foraging party made the mistake of breaking into the splendid old mansion one night on one of their raids. They ran into an experience none of them ever forgot. No sooner had they forced the front door and entered, torches held high for illumination, than they were set upon by a whirling creature with a mane of flowing, red hair who was dressed in a long black gown.

The apparition laid about her with an oar and soon had the British in utter confusion. As if blown by some tremendous gust of wind, all the torches were extinguished in the same instant. The terrified sailors began to strike out blindly with their knives, seriously wounding several of their company. When they finally did fumble their way to the door, they beat a hasty retreat, carrying their wounded with them. Back on shipboard, they spread the word of their eerie experience, and never again was a foraging party to visit Spriggs' Luck.

Following the war, the fine old home was sold and resold many times, sometimes to people who were delighted with their purchase and sometimes to others who were terrified and wanted to get rid of it as quickly as possible. The difference was Jerushia. If she found the new owners to be lazy and inefficient housekeepers who let her home become run down and dilapidated, she would make life miserable for them with appearances and manifestations and sleepless nights until she finally drove them away. If, on the other hand, she saw that the owners took good care of Spriggs' Luck and kept it in a good state of repair, she would give them no trouble whatsoever. She had loved that house during her life, and she was not about to desert it now to unappreciative tenants.

Not only did she love and protect her former home;

she also continued her interest in the islanders. Many are the tales of her help given to poor fishermen in their time of danger or of need. Often a wife in childbirth was comforted and soothed by the presence of that six-foot feminine figure with the shock of red hair. Her people did not and they do not fear her. They believe in her and respect and love her to this day for the aid and comfort she has brought a hardy, but often underprivileged, people.

For generations Spriggs' Luck stood as an inspiration and historic landmark in Portsmouth Town, but in time its luck ran out and it met the fate of all man-made structures on these Outer Banks.

It was the big hurricane, then called an equinoctial storm, of 1899 that destroyed most of what sea-born Jerushia had fought so long and so well to preserve. All during that historic storm, according to established folk memory, the natives heard wild cries of despair as the raging winds ripped and tore at the structure. The screams and the howling of the wind reached an awful crescendo at the same instant. At that second, Spriggs' Luck collapsed with a mighty roar. Board was torn from board, and the wreckage was whipped and strewn across the entire width of the island. The wind-driven tide pounded against the foundations and scattered the fragments of wreckage even farther inland.

It is hard to imagine the fury of such a wind gone insane. Facing into the wind, it is impossible to breathe, and if one puts his back to the blow, it seems as though one's very lungs will be sucked from his body by that awful pressure. Tiny straws are actually blown through the trunks of small trees, so awful is the force of the moving air. Strongly built houses just disappear as if they were made of cards, and the whole appearance of a region is drastically altered in the winking of an eye. Such a storm was the 1899 disaster.

When the blow had spent its fury and the winds and seas had once again subsided, all that was left of the ancient building was the stub of a brick chimney and the massive hearthstone, now at ground level, that marked the final resting place of the old pirate. And that is all that remains today of Spriggs' Luck, now called "Brigand's Luck" by some.

Sea-born Woman did not vanish with the structure, however. Full many a sailor has stood to the wheel of his boat trying to steer a safe course through fog or driving rain to enter Ocracoke Inlet and has suddenly become aware of a tall, willowy figure standing by his side, mahogany hair floating free in the wind and long arm and forefinger pointing the way to safe passage. Still the tall, graceful figure can be seen on rare occasions as she moves about that marble slab. Sometimes, they say, if you listen very carefully and remain very still, you can hear the faint sound of gay laughter and the music of long, long ago.

The Night the *Crissie Wright* Came Ashore

One of the things for which the Outer Banks are famous
is the mildness of the climate. Influenced by the nearness
of the warm waters of the Gulf Stream, these islands are
usually pleasantly warm in the winter and pleasantly cool

in the summer. But, as is the case with most rules, there are exceptions to this general statement. When it does become cold on the Outer Banks, it can be a bone-chilling cold.

When one of these unusual spells of frigid weather sets in, especially if it is complicated by a storm with gale-force winds, you are likely to hear reference to an event which has long been remembered. The story has been told and retold until it has become a part of the very language of the region. Thus, when you hear anyone around Harker's Island, Beaufort Town, or Morehead City remark, "It's as cold as the night the *Crissie Wright* came ashore," you know he is speaking about a regionally famous historical event. This disaster took place almost a hundred years ago. It was so horrible that the very phrases *"Crissie Wright* time" or "when the *Crissie Wright* came ashore" have burned themselves into the everyday speech of the people.

Our story begins in mid-October of the year 1885, when it was actually spring in the lovely capital of Brazil, Rio de Janeiro. Already, the days in that South American metropolis were getting longer, and people were looking forward to the long, lazy summer days to come in December, January, and February. The sun was "moving south" as old earth began its annual tilt to divide the seasons between the hemispheres. Securely moored to one of the docks in the broad mouth of the "River of January," which makes up a good portion of the splendid Rio Harbor, was the American sailing ship, the *Crissie Wright.* The vessel was a thing of beauty as well as utility, a three-masted schooner of some eight hundred tons burden. She was a fine representative of the growing fleet of American sailing ships which was already dominating international trade.

The ship's seven crewmen whiled away their time in Rio by the sea, while their good ship was loaded with a full eight hundred tons of phosphate for delivery to New York. It mattered little to them that they would be sailing northward into the approaching winter, or that they would be passing the North Carolina coast, with its dreaded Graveyard of the Sea, at a time when they could expect the worst possible weather. After more than a year, they were going home! Every man jack of them was anxious to see the loading completed, the lines that bound them to this foreign shore cast off, and the native pilot dropped off into his little pilot boat as they passed the Rio Harbor bar and made their way into the South Atlantic.

Departure day finally arrived in mid-October. The *Crissie Wright*, loaded to her full capacity and completely stocked with provisions, took her leave of Rio de Janeiro. Captain Jeb Collins ordered the graceful, long blue pennant called the "Blue Peter," which signified that a ship was homeward bound, run up to the masthead. There it immediately began to snap and pop in the brisk, favorable breeze. It seemed a good omen for a fast and safe trip.

Captain Collins was a typical Yankee skipper in his mid-forties. Born to the sea, he had made sailing ships his life's vocation, and he was a very competent mariner and skipper. Normally mild mannered, he was, nevertheless, very strict when his ship was under weigh. He brooked no delay in carrying out his orders for the safety and well-being of his ship and crew. All things considered, Captain Collins was one of the best in the business. His spirits were high as the *Crissie Wright* made her way out into the blue Atlantic. It had been a profitable voyage for the owners, with cargoes both on the trip out and on this return voyage. If all went well, the crew could count on a bonus; but, above all else, each man just wanted to be back home.

They ran northward under fair skies and with favorable winds, and the temperature grew hotter and hotter as they approached the equator. As they passed into the Northern Hemisphere, the days gradually became colder, as they raced to meet winter head-on. The weather held generally good for sailing, though, until they picked up the Gulf Stream off Cuba and added the northward thrust of that mighty river in the ocean to their own sail power. She was a good ship, the *Crissie Wright*, and she made good time, even though she lay low in the water from the weight of her capacity cargo.

By the time they were off Charleston, South Carolina, the weather really began to worsen, and Second Mate Sam Grover sounded the warning of foul weather conditions ahead. Though Mister Grover's specialty was navigation, he had also developed a very keen sense of the weather and could predict it with remarkable accuracy. His mates called him the ship's second barometer, and he took a great deal of pride and pleasure in the title. "It's going to be bad, mates," he growled. "There's something real big brewing between us and home."

As they arrived off the coast of North Carolina and passed Cape Fear, they were still making fairly good speed.

THE FLAMING SHIP OF OCRACOKE

The wind, while nearing full gale strength, held fair for them, and they boiled along at a good rate. It was only when the huge Welsh First Mate, John Blackman, alerted the skipper to the fact that the entire bow was disappearing beneath the increasing ocean swells that Captain Collins began to ease his ship to take the strain off her. Blackman's seamanship and judgment were impeccable and tempered by years of experience and a deep love for the sea. The skipper, after consulting Mister Blackman, decided to press on, making as much "northing" as possible under shortened sail. After all, they had all been in much harder blows than this and had come through all right. Their ship was sound and seaworthy, and the crew was experienced, even to the young ship's carpenter, James Boswell, and the cabin boy, Chester Simmons. If necessary, even Cookie Johnson, the rotund ship's cook, could be counted on to do the work of two good able-bodied seamen. Though he was "encased in blubber," according to his mates, he was a powerfully built man and a knowledgeable seaman.

Some miles to the south of Cape Lookout, the *Crissie Wright* was running under shortened sail before a very strong and gusty wind out of the south-southeast. A glance at a chart of the North Carolina coastline reveals that Cape Lookout, on the extreme tip of Core Banks, extends in a huge hook landward, toward Shackleford Banks, creating what is called Lookout Bight and forming an almost landlocked shelter from the wind and weather. For the schooner, of course, the wind was directly "onshore" for Shackleford Banks, behind which the broad, calm waters of Back Sound formed what has been called one of the greatest natural harbors in the world.

The *Crissie Wright* was just eighty-four days out of Rio and well ahead of schedule, so Captain Collins decided to make a run for the shelter of Lookout Bight and there ride out the worsening storm. Seeking the advice of his first and second officers, Blackman and Grover, Captain Collins called a hurried meeting. The alternative, they knew, would be to "wear ship," head out into that screaming wind and cold in an effort to gain sea room, and try to make passage around the dreaded Cape Hatteras in the middle of a winter storm with a ship already low in the water. The vote was unanimous in favor of a run for the safety of Lookout Bight; it was obviously the prudent thing to do.

But fate stepped in, and one of those totally unforeseeable quirks took place which, all too frequently, alter the fortunes and rule the destinies of seafaring men.

The *Crissie Wright* was running for her life, with the howling gale almost directly on her starboard beam. She was handling well and was standing about easterly on the starboard tack. Her sails were drawing beautifully and she was headed straight as an arrow for Lookout Bight when, suddenly, the wind became baffling and variable and even more blustery. As though slapped by a huge hand, the gallant vessel groaned in her travail and lay over almost on her starboard beam ends. Then, as the wind flawed again, she shifted the other way until she was almost lying on her port beam ends. As the schooner righted herself the second time, the full force of that gale caught her sails aback. The main brace supporting the large main-mast snapped like an overtightened violin string, and the huge mast came toppling down on the deck, bringing a welter of sails and standing and running rigging with it.

The beautiful *Crissie Wright* was doomed. She lay dead in the water with that huge mast trailing overside, and she would not answer her helm. The only hope now was to drop both anchors and pray that they would hold the ship off that lee shore. This was promptly done. The anchors bit into the ocean bottom all right and brought the stricken vessel's head up into the gale wind. For a short time the anchors held, and a flicker of hope arose. They might, yet, manage to survive. Then, to his horror, the Captain discovered that the sight-bearings he was taking on various points ashore were changing. The ship was moving! The anchors were dragging, and the *Crissie Wright* was being driven, stern first, toward the raging surf of Shackleford Banks.

On the second sand reef, which was about two hundred yards offshore, the *Crissie Wright* finally ran aground. Then, like a tired old lady, she gradually broached in the direction of her port side and lay grounded on that reef. Every wave breaking over her starboard side swept all the way over her decks, from starboard to port. The sea water was actually freezing, and each breaker added to the sheet of ice steadily forming on the portions of the schooner still above the water.

With hope all but gone, Captain Collins ordered his crew to take what refuge they could find by climbing partway up the foremast and lashing themselves to what rigging was left. Obedient and well-disciplined to the end, they obeyed his order without hesitation or question. Up the slippery foremast all seven of them climbed, in an effort to get above the reach of the icy waves. They lashed themselves with rope as securely as numbed fingers would allow and waited for they knew not what. The sea was a boiling cauldron of mad waves under the lash of that ever-changing wind.

Ashore, the plight of the desperate seamen had not gone unnoticed. From the little fishing and whaling villages of Wade's Shores, Windsor's Lump, and Guthrie's Hammock, the Bankers congregated on the beach and built a huge bonfire to give what cheer they could to the shipwreck victims. It is told that, three times that afternoon and early evening, they tried to put a pulling or rowing boat through the raging surf. All three times, the angry ocean literally threw boat and oarsmen back onto the beach. On the third try, the boat was stove in by the force of the blow as it hit the sand. One of the would-be rescuers suffered a broken leg, and two others were nearly drowned. It was hopeless.

All night long, the Bankers kept that bonfire going. Hour after freezing hour, they shouted words of encouragement into the gale and sang hymns at the tops of their voices. They prayed to Almighty God for help—some kind of help—for the stricken seamen out there in the darkness. Seafaring people themselves, they knew the terrors of the deep.

That night the wind shifted abruptly to the northwest and increased in velocity, and it became even colder. The lowest recorded temperature in nearby, sheltered Beaufort Town that night was exactly eight degrees. God alone knows what it dropped to on that exposed beach at Shackleford Banks.

The next day the wind increased still more. Finally, the watchers on the beach saw Captain Collins apparently lose his grip on the foremast and fall headlong into the raging sea. His body was never found. Soon after, First Mate Blackman and Able Seaman Dozier untied themselves from the mast and made a dash for the forecastle, obviously in the hope of finding some warmth and shelter from the killing cold. They ran awkwardly on numbed legs and made no more than half the distance they hoped to go when a huge comber swept them both off the wreck to instant death in the raging, freezing sea. The other four managed to get forward, somehow, as the ship's stern began to settle lower into the sea. They huddled together and wrapped themselves as best they could into the stiff folds of the jib sail.

The frantic people on shore could stand it no longer. They resolved to try, yet again, to get to the ship, even though they well knew the attempt to be apparently suicidal. In times of crisis, real men seem to gather added, almost superhuman, strength to meet seemingly impossible tasks. But to launch another boat through that surf gone mad, when three former attempts had failed, seemed little short of insanity. But try they did. And they succeeded, though to this day no one can say how they did it.

Captain Seef Willis had come over during the night, and at first light he sent back for his whaling boat and crew at Diamond City. In a very short time, the seasoned whaling crew came, dragging with them the surfboat used to pursue and kill the giant whales offshore. In the face of impossible odds and with practically no chance of success, those unsung heroes put that whale boat through the surf and were able to pull alongside the wrecked *Crissie Wright*.

Only the fat cook, Johnson, was still alive. The other three, Grover, Boswell, and Simmons, were literally frozen stiff. To this day, it is claimed that, if Johnson had not had such a thick layer of fat over most of his body, he too would have frozen and died. It is believed that his obesity actually saved his life.

The three bodies and the half-frozen cook were brought back to shore in another miracle of seamanship. Cookie was wrapped in blankets and thawed out very slowly right there on the beach. He was not allowed too near the bonfire, because his rescuers knew that too much heat, too quickly, would prove fatal.

The story goes that Cookie had to be forcibly restrained from throwing himself into the warmth of the leaping flames. It is certain that, for a long while there on that exposed beach, he was out of his mind and raving. They held him and turned him slowly like a huge roast before the fire, until feeling began to return to his limbs and sanity to his mind. To ease his torture and stop his screaming, they plied him with rum, until he was finally led away, almost anaesthetized, and put to bed under a mountain of blankets. But he alone, of the entire ship's company, survived that terrible ordeal.

Down to this point, the tellers and the retellers of this familiar story are in substantial agreement as to the facts. From here, the accounts differ somewhat.

B. M. C. Eugene Pond, U. S. Coast Guard, Retired, and

a native of this region, says that the three bodies were buried there in the sand on Shackleford Banks and that Cookie Johnson recovered completely, went back to Boston, and probably shipped out again as cook on another vessel.

Graydon Paul, another knowledgeable native, insists that the three bodies were brought back to Beaufort and were buried there in an unmarked common grave not thirty feet from the spot where the British naval officer was buried standing upright. Mr. Paul also says that the ship's cook never completely recovered either in mind or in body. He says that Cookie went to Charleston, South Carolina, but very soon returned to Shackleford Banks, where he died of a heart attack.

Well, whichever of these fine gentlemen has the true facts, the fate of the *Crissie Wright* and the manner of her dying are matters of history. Down to this very day, when a coastlander tells you, "It's as cold as the night the *Crissie Wright* came ashore," you can very well know that he is telling you that it's just about as cold as it can possibly get. Thus have the tragic deaths of those brave seamen burned (or frozen) a new expression into the very language of a people. This, too, is part and parcel of the wonderful heritage of the Outer Banks.

The Female of the Species

In the early days of this country, North Carolina's coastal region was the main theater of operations for many a well-known pirate. Some, like the famous Blackbeard, were admired and looked up to as heroes by the poorer settlers.

Others were greatly feared because of their reputations for cruelty and sadism. But none of this motley "Brotherhood of the Sea" were quite so colorful as the two famous female pirates of the day, Anne Bonny and Mary Read. Each was, in a sense, a product of coastal Carolina in the early days of colonization.

Anne Bonny was born in County Cork, Ireland, the illegitimate daughter of a wealthy lawyer and his wife's maid. Because of some trouble, possibly political in nature, Bonny and the maid took Anne and fled across the Atlantic to the New World, leaving his wife in Ireland.

When they arrived, Bonny purchased an extensive estate on the beautiful, broad waters of the Neuse River just below New Berne in what is now Craven County, and he prospered from the start. He was industrious as well as highly intelligent, so he soon achieved considerable status as a lawyer, merchant, and farmer. Much of his business was in trading with the many ships that plied the Neuse River from the nearby Atlantic sea lanes. He even seemed to have mended his political fortunes to the point where he became magistrate, and his beautiful home became one of the showplaces of the area in which he lived.

When Anne's mother died, the girl naturally moved into her place as mistress of the household, directing the several servants who were apprenticed or "bound" to the place in exchange for having been given free passage to the new land of opportunity. Whether it was the lack of maternal supervision and loss of the softening effect of a mother's love or whether it was just Anne's basic nature coming to the surface will never be known, but the girl soon developed into a self-centered, strong-willed tyrant in her own little sphere. She brooked absolutely no opposition to her will. She lorded her authority over the women servants, in particular, and missed no opportunity to vent her spite on anyone she considered beneath her station.

According to contemporary accounts of the times, Anne Bonny, even as a girl, possessed "a fierce and corageous" temper, which she took little pains to conceal. Reliable local tradition insists that, when a frightened maidservant once accidentally spilled hot soup over one of her favorite dinner gowns, the enraged Anne sprang from her seat, seized one of the dirks lying on a nearby mantel, and disemboweled the luckless maid with one savage, twisting slash. Squire Bonny was finally able to hush up the killing by the judicious use of a considerable amount of his wealth, but Anne's reputation spread about the countryside like wildfire.

In spite of her reputation for cruelty, Anne had many suitors among the local gentry. Although she was known to be of a violent disposition, she was also the only child of a very wealthy father. It was presumed that she would someday inherit all of the family possessions. Besides, man has always toyed with the idea that he could somehow succeed in taming the shrew, even though others before him had failed.

And what a shrew for the taming Anne was! Tall for a woman and almost manly in her movements, she was, nevertheless, wide-hipped and deep-bosomed, broad of shoulder and strong of thigh, a veritable Amazon. A wild sort of beauty she had, with a wealth of shining, jet-black hair and large, flashing blue eyes betokening a spirit that no man had ever been able to tame. She was a superb horsewoman and an expert in the use of sword and pistol, the result of patient training by her doting, though sometimes bewildered, father.

This was the prize contended for by many of the young Carolinians who lived thereabout. Although they all professed undying affection and desire for her, and although several even went so far as to fight duels over her, she treated them all with amused contempt. "Milksops," she called them, "pretty boys," and "fortune hunters." She was the ultimate challenge to every mother's son of them, and they resented her cool disdain.

Considering her poor opinion of most men, the manner of her falling in love was most unusual. On her part, it was love at first sight, and the object of her affection was a plain, ordinary sailor from one of the merchant ships that had called at her father's wharf. He was a reformed pirate who had taken the King's Pardon, and he owned nothing in this world but the marlinspike stuck in his belt and the sailor's clothes he stood in. But he was young, healthy, and handsome, and Anne was much taken with him. Who can say what magic or what chemistry first attracts a maid to a man? At first he ran like a scared rabbit from Anne's bold, open approach. He had never seen a woman like her. His shipmates soon pointed out to him the many advantages of a rich wife such as Squire Bonny's daughter. Thereafter, the courtship moved at a goodly pace with overtures on both sides.

When the day came that they were sure they could no longer go on without each other, the young couple went to John Bonny and asked his permission to marry. At this preposterous request, all the pent-up worry and frustration this Irish gentleman felt about his daughter broke loose. His hitherto repressed Irish temper flared into full flame. In no uncertain terms, he denied their request and ordered the young sailor off his premises, never to return on threat of violent death. Shouting imprecations at the top of his voice against penniless fortune hunters, he ordered his daughter to her room to stay until he gave her leave to come forth. Then, pistol in hand, he escorted the terrified suitor back to his vessel and aided his ascent of the gang-plank with a mighty kick.

Alas for Squire Bonny! Did he really think that he could thus thwart either true love or the iron will of his daughter? Even as the elder Bonny proceeded to quench the heat of his anger by drinking himself into oblivion, Anne busied herself upstairs gathering up all the money and other valuables she could lay her hands on. Having collected a considerable sum, she silently escaped down the roof which slanted gently almost to the ground out-side her bedroom window. She then quietly made her way to her lover's ship which, under orders of the Squire, was even then preparing to cast off and be on its way.

By spending only a small part of her valuables, Anne was able to persuade the captain to alter his plans and to take them down the Neuse River and through the ancient thoroughfare by Cedar Island to Beaufort Town, where they were married in the little chapel. In Beaufort, she purchased a small but strong coastal schooner with the re-mainder of her dower wealth. While the little schooner was being outfitted and loaded with cargo, the honey-mooning couple spent a few happy weeks at a combined inn and tavern in Beaufort called the Inn of the Three Horseshoes, a fairly new hostelry operated by a man named Jack Read and his young wife of a few months, Mary. It was a happy time, and it seemed that the very name of the inn presaged a bright future for the young couple. The elder Bonny did not put in an appearance to mar their happiness. The Inn of the Three Horseshoes became their first home, and each of them felt that nothing could possibly arise to threaten their happiness.

At last all was ready. Their graceful little ship was completely fitted out for sea and held a cargo of tobacco and naval stores consigned for delivery in Boston. Although it has always been a tradition of the sea that it is bad luck to have any woman aboard a ship, Anne could not bring herself to part with her new husband, so she sailed with him on the first voyage of the new ship.

On a bright and sparkling day, the little schooner took advantage of a tide just past its peak and sailed smartly out of Beaufort Harbor, around Shark Shoal, and out the inlet into the blue-green Atlantic. The crewmen, who had been hired in Beaufort Town, seemed to know their duties. They handled the sails and the rigging smartly as the bridegroom leaned expertly against the mahogany wheel, his radiant bride reclining gracefully against the lee rail of the afterdeck.

As the sails bellied taut with the favorable breeze and the immortal song of the sea began to sing from the forefoot and along the water line of the little craft, everything seemed almost too perfect. Little did Anne know, nor could she tell, the horror that awaited them just over the horizon. The fate that now hurried toward them was destined so to change her entire life that her name would go down in history, alongside that of the infamous Lucrezia Borgia of Italy, as one of the most cruel and bloodthirsty female creatures known to the memory of man. In that hour of beginnings, though, no shadow of impending fate spoiled the mood of the travelers as they cleared Beaufort Inlet and set their course to join the Gulf Stream as it swept northward toward Diamond Shoals. Every prospect was auspicious, and hearts were high.

About midafternoon of the second day out, as the Bight of Hatteras came into view, a lively brigantine burst into sight, racing from behind the cape point before the gentle northeast breeze. Every square sail of her, from the big mainsail right on up to the topgallant sails, was drawing beautifully.

Few sights are more beautiful than that of a sailing ship handled as she should be handled and sailed right up to the full of her potential. But the honeymooners scarcely had time to catch their breath in appreciation of this beautiful scene before they saw another detail which caused their blood to run cold. Atop the mainmast, just above the straining, white topgallant sail, was a huge, rectangular, black flag bearing the outline in red of a human skeleton. The very worst had befallen the bride and groom. Here was the greatest danger they could have encountered, the pirate ship *Fancy* under the command of the mad Captain Edward Low. Low was known the seven seas over as an insane seafaring genius, whose chief delight was inflicting torture and slow death on each member of the luckless crews of the ships he captured.

Early in his piratical career, the left side of Low's face

had been laid open to the bone and teeth by the vicious sabre slash of an adversary. After the battle, the ship's surgeon had tried in vain to sew up the ugly wound. The pirate, by then roaring drunk as the result of his efforts to find both an antiseptic and an anaesthetic in the rum bottle, would not lie still. Crazy with pain and rum, he knocked the surgeon senseless and tried to sew up his own face with the curved needle. He made such a mess of it that, forever after, his head resembled the caricature of a skull. The yellowed teeth and bone shone through the slit cheek in a horrible grimace even when his face was relaxed, giving him an expression of deadly menace.

There seems to be no doubt at all that the pirate captain was violently insane. Consequently, he was one of the most dreaded robbers and murderers who roved the sea lanes of that day. The very sight of his red skeleton flag struck terror to the hearts of most seafarers. It is said that this capacity to terrify his victims often resulted in the abject surrender of many vessels to his flag without any fight whatsoever.

Now, Anne Bonny's new husband was no fool. He knew instantly that their only hope lay in precipitate flight, and he and his little crew very smartly "wore ship" and fled in the opposite direction in a desperate effort to run into shallower water over some nearby shoals. The brigantine was the larger and faster ship, however, and she already had considerable momentum or "way" on. The pursuit turned out to be no race.

Before the fascinated gaze of a score of natives on the shore, the *Fancy* cut off the little schooner from the shoal, came alongside, threw huge grappling hooks over her rail, and proceeded to send a boarding party onto her decks. When the brief resistance of the crew was overcome and the two ships were firmly lashed together, the mad captain himself boarded Anne's vessel.

The scene of inhuman torture that followed is better left undescribed, although the descendants of those on shore talk about it to this day. Anne Bonny was stripped to the waist and tied securely to the mast of her ship. She was the butt of many an obscene and cruel jest as the pirates forced her to look on, during intermittent periods of consciousness, while the surviving crewmen and her husband were slowly and brutally killed. As the frightened and horrified fishermen on the island watched from hiding in the yaupon and scrub cedar, the lifeless bodies of the crew were thrown over the rail into the midst of an increasing number of sharks, which were attracted by the scent of blood in the water.

Anne's little vessel was looted, stripped of her running rigging and fittings, and set afire to burn and drift with the tide. Anne herself was taken prisoner aboard the pirate ship, which soon thereafter returned to that nest of pirates known as the island of New Providence in the Bahamas.

This lovely island contained a most amazing government of, by, and for pirates. The Brotherhood of the Sea maintained some semblance of order in disorder. There were fights and duels aplenty among individual freebooters, but strict loyalty was maintained to the charter of the place. Each ship's company was a little community within the general community, and each captain was responsible for the conduct of his men. In disputes between crews, a jury from the crews of other ships was hastily summoned to sit in judgment. Strangely enough, a rough sort of justice was achieved, and there was little quarreling with the decisions of the juries. Only the captain of a ship could pass judgment of death upon one of his crew, and that only with the agreement of a majority of the sailors on that particular ship. The division of the spoils between individual crew members was decided by a strict formula to which all ships adhered, and a percentage of the loot was paid to maintain the stronghold.

Released ashore on New Providence as a free woman and left to perish or survive by her own wits, Anne soon became a well-known figure in the community. Although many people believe she never fully regained her right mind after the massacre off Hatteras, her will to live was strong. Anne not only subsisted; she also became one of the favorites of the pirate captains for whom New Providence was the nearest thing to a home port that they ever knew. The island itself possessed a spirit, a sort of flavor, that was not entirely disagreeable to the wild, boisterous spirit of Anne Bonny. Here she found men who could match her own cruelty. They were her equals in physical bravery, and they lived and died with a swagger and an *élan* that she found completely fascinating and often admirable.

One of the moving spirits in this den of buccaneers was a worthy named John James Rackham. It was this same Rackham who connived with the famous Blackbeard to maroon the pirate Captain Charles Vane on a lonely island so that Rackham, Vane's former mate, could steal Vane's ship and sail in convoy with Blackbeard. Honor among thieves? Well, Rackham's outwitting of Captain Vane was related with shouts of laughter all over the pirate world, and the trickster was thereby enabled to cut quite a figure in that lawless society. After obtaining command of his own ship in this doubly piratical way, Rackham began to affect britches made of bright calico cloth. These became his trademark, and he soon became known as "Calico Jack" Rackham.

Anne Bonny and Calico Jack were attracted to each other from the very first. Anne was growing weary of the humdrum life ashore, and one of the conditions she interposed when Calico Jack proposed marriage was that he take her with him whenever he went a-pirating.

It is unclear whether any person even remotely connected with the church was present at the pirate wedding, but a wedding there was. A wilder, more flamboyant and bacchanalian week was never seen, even on the island of New Providence. Apparently, there were rules and customs that applied to pirate weddings, although they were quite different from those employed under more normal circumstances. The two principals finally stood up and faced each other on the sandy beach and repeated to each other an approximation of the wedding vows. All hands seemed to consider the marriage quite binding, however; from that time forward, it was accepted without question that Calico Jack and Anne were husband and wife.

Rackham kept his prenuptial promise to the letter. Maybe he was afraid not to. Anyway, the arrangement resulted in one of the most fantastic situations imaginable. Anne not only sailed with Rackham on his piratical cruises; she also took delight in donning a man's attire and participating in the actual hand-to-hand fighting and loot-ing with as much gusto as any member of the crew. There were dark mutterings among some members of that crew about defying the ancient taboo against a woman on ship-board. Many were the predictions of disaster sure to fol-low if the practice was continued.

It had its pleasanter side, though. Anne was a thorough-ly dependable and trustworthy ally to have on a boarding party, and the meals she occasionally cooked for the crew were delicious beyond anything they normally had on board ship. Besides, Anne and Calico Jack were without doubt the two most deadly swordsmen in the entire motley aggregation. It could well have cost you your life to give offense to either of them.

Some historians believe that, all this time, Anne was hoping against hope for an encounter with the crazy Captain Edward Low and a chance to even the score with him. He was not a member of the New Providence society, and they never met at sea, so that chance was denied her.

There was one instance and, so far as we know, only one, of near-infidelity to mar this somewhat idyllic, if un-lawful, relationship dedicated to violence and crime. Be-cause of the inevitable toll of constant combat, Rackham's crew, at one time, was reduced in number to the point where it was difficult to man the ship in a storm and where the outcome of a battle was becoming more and more doubtful. Being, above all else, a realist, Calico Jack then began to attack somewhat smaller ships and to offer the conquered crewmen of those ships the choice of walking the plank or joining the pirate crew with the promise of a full share of the booty. Understandably, many of those previously honest seamen took the blood oath and joined the Rackham crew, and many of them developed quite an aptitude for piracy and infused new energy into the company.

One such converted merchant seaman was a young sailor who signed in blood with the name "M. Read." Lithe and agile, and with the smooth, beardless cheek normally associated with the young, this sunburned youth immediately caught the fancy of Anne Bonny Rackham. There was a gentleness and a grace about this new crew member that stood out in sharp contrast to the bearing of the others. With her accustomed directness and openness, Anne began to pursue and to attempt to court, in a hundred different ways, this new object of her fascination. The fact that M. Read seemed to shy away from her and avoid her advances only fanned the flame of her interest and made her redouble her efforts.

The climax of this very one-sided affair occurred one warm, starlit night when the pirate ship was anchored in the natural harbor of a beautiful Caribbean island. Most of the crew had gone ashore with Rackham in search of pigs, which they seized from the natives. The pirates then proceeded to "boucan" the half-wild porkers right there on the beach.

Now, to boucan a pig was the very same thing as barbecuing it, and the result of the boucan was a delicious gustatory treat of which pirates all over that region were very fond. In fact, boucans were so frequent that the pirates eventually became known as "boucan-eers," and this term later became, through much usage, simply "buccaneers." Thus, a buccaneer was a heavily-armed sea robber who came ashore on an island, stole the natives' pigs, and barbecued them on the beach. The boucan was usually concluded with a prolonged drinking spree which left senseless and snoring on the sand all but the few assigned to guard the pirate group.

And so it was on the night of which we speak. Only Anne Bonny and three or four of the crew, M. Read among them, remained on board the ship.

Knowing that M. Read was assigned the anchor watch and was thus unable to leave the deck of the pirate ship, Anne waited until the few members of the crew left aboard had settled down to sleep. All was calm and serene; the moon cast a beautiful glow over the deck, and Anne felt that her golden moment of opportunity was at hand. With a soft fire in her eyes, Anne Bonny moved in for the capture.

Taking a seat beside the handsome, young, smooth-skinned sailor, the ardent lady pirate began to make a complete confession of her feelings for her younger shipmate. Quite eloquently did Anne argue her case, and quite directly and boldly, as was her wont. She was apparently oblivious to the danger that she might be overheard by a wakeful member of the crew and her conduct reported to Rackham.

All this while young Read remained silent, indicating only by an occasional nervous movement of the head or a desperate sidelong glance overside that Anne's words were even heard or, if heard, were making any impression whatsoever. Finally, with a sigh of resignation, young Read turned so that each was looking directly into the other's face and made a disclosure that must have shaken Anne to her very corset stays!

M. Read was a woman, also!

Then, in a veritable torrent of words, Mary Read told how it had come about that she was also dressed in men's clothing and carrying out the duties of a merchant seaman. Now she also became oblivious to the danger of being overheard. Now it was the silent one who felt the compulsion to talk and talk and talk until her full story was known to the other woman sitting there in stunned silence by her side. The tale she told was, if anything, more incredible than Anne Bonny's had been.

Soon after her birth in England, Mary Read's parents had decided to play a trick on her paternal grandmother by concealing the fact that the baby was a girl instead of the male heir the old lady had hopefully expected. Feeling that little Mary would be disinherited if it were learned that she was a girl, the parents did everything in their power to carry out the deception. They dressed her in boys' clothing, gave her the nickname "Jack," and insisted that she learn and practice boys' games and pastimes.

The deceit might have worked with the desired result except for the fact that the old lady lived on and on, and her health got better with age. What had started as a calculated fraud resulted in the development of a muscular, active, and profane counterfeit of a young man of the lower middle class. Grandma really had cause to believe that her grandchild was a virile, strapping young man, and she made occasional generous gifts to this favorite grandchild, but the bulk of her estate she kept in order to see to her own comfort and security.

Bored with her life in England, Mary then decided that, if she was going to have the name of a boy, she might as well have some of the fun boys are supposed to have. She hoped that her grandmother would believe all the more strongly that she was the male heir everyone assumed her to be. Running away from home, the strapping youth enlisted in the infantry in Flanders and served out a full enlistment undetected. Disliking the constant marching, she then shipped out on an English merchant ship and got her first taste of life at sea which, from her standpoint as a cabin "boy," she found less than attractive.

After a year at sea, her ship docked again in Flanders, and she promptly jumped ship and reenlisted in the Flemish armed forces, this time in a regiment of cavalry. Then, she felt she was in an occupation that suited her very well. She came to love the thrilling massed charges of the full brigade of horses, the stealthy thrill of picket duty on horseback, and the satisfying sense of being needed as she rubbed down her horse and cared for him and fed him. Once again, her true sex went completely undetected. In those days, the acceptable standards of personal hygiene and sanitation were vastly different from minimum standards today. Even so, it is remarkable that her masquerade could have succeeded as long as it did and that "Jack Hawkins," guidon bearer for a regiment of horse, should have gone so long unrevealed.

In the end, it was her own feminine nature which betrayed her. A dashing, handsome young cavalryman named Jack Read, a man who seemed to epitomize the traits she admired in men, was transferred into her regiment. The better she knew him, the better she liked him. In due course, she confessed both her true sex and her affection for him. Read must have been among the most startled of men. Cavalrymen, however, traditionally have a fine sense of balance, and when he recovered his aplomb, he discovered that he reciprocated Mary's feelings.

Laying their plans well, the two sweethearts deserted their regiment just in time to catch a ship bound for the Carolina colonies. They were married on shipboard by the Captain and traveled finally to Beaufort Town in North Carolina, where they set up a combination inn and tavern. They soon accumulated a fine stable of horses, and, to show their love for things equine, they named their establishment "The Three Horseshoes." It was the very inn at which Anne Bonny and her bridegroom had spent their honeymoon after running away from Anne's father. Now the two women's paths had crossed again, but under what different circumstances!

Mary swore that she remembered Anne and her young husband and that she had remarked, at the time, on what a handsome couple they made. She had not known what had finally become of Anne until the first day she saw her in woman's dress on the pirate ship. From that day on, she had been much too frightened to reveal herself.

Mary Read's husband had died in Beaufort and, for a while, she had operated the Inn of the Three Horseshoes by herself. But the work was more than she could handle alone, and the care of the several horses was a burden to her. She longed for the old, carefree life of the sea and thought of it more and more often. When she finally had a chance to sell the inn and the horses for a good price, she sold out, lock, stock, and barrel. Traveling to Portsmouth Island, she once again donned the male attire she knew so well and signed on a merchant ship as a seaman. M. Read remained unsuspected and undiscovered until Anne's interest forced her disclosure.

Thereafter, the two women became good friends, and Anne did not betray her new friend's secret until Calico Jack's jealousy made him suspicious of the tanned young sailor with whom Anne was often seen engaging in animated conversation. Poor Rackham! He had no way of knowing that it was only "woman talk" between them, so he confronted the pair one day, dagger in hand, fully prepared to do violence to M. Read. After first swearing him to secrecy, Anne and Mary revealed her secret to the pirate captain. Thunderstruck and speechless in his amazement, Calico Jack could only cover his confusion with roars of laughter.

Rackham kept his vow of secrecy, and M. Read was able to keep her place as a member of the crew, neither asking nor giving favor in the performance of all the tasks involved in the business of sea robbery. Legend has it that Anne Bonny and M. Read frequently engaged in fencing matches with each other and so sharpened their skills with the dirk, the sword, and the pistol that the other crewmen held them, not only in respect, but in absolute fear. They never seemed to quarrel between themselves. Perhaps each had too much respect for the deadly skills of the other, or perhaps there was a bond of sympathy between them.

Mary Read was apparently content to continue her

sham and live the life of a pirate crewman on board ship. When the buccaneers went ashore, though, she could not join fully in the roistering and wild, drunken celebrating that went on. There was too much danger, she thought, that she would inadvertently reveal her true nature. Thus, Mary lived a rather lonely life when all around her were whooping it up, and she began to long, once more, for a more normal, womanly existence, even as a pirate. After all, Anne Bonny was a woman and was accepted without question, in spite of the ancient superstition that a woman was bad luck aboard a ship. But Anne had a husband, and that seemed to make all the difference.

It seemed as though the gods of the sea took pity on Mary's plight. On the very next expedition, Rackham's ship captured a vessel manned by a youngish crew of better than average sailors. Appealing to the pirate captain, Mary chose one of the captured sailors as her full share of the prize. This was sometimes done by pirates who, thenceforward, held these "slaves" as enforced servants until it suited their pleasure to free them, sometimes years later. Mary had other ideas in mind for her prize. Imagine the astonishment of her slave when Mary got him ashore, disclosed her true sex to him, and then told him she intended to make him her husband!

History does not tell us what, if any, alternative was offered the young captive, but whatever it was, he chose marriage to Mary Read. From all accounts, this fellow was a gentle, mild sort of person, more given to books and philosophy than to burning and looting. Now Mary considered that she was almost on an equal footing with Anne Bonny Rackham. Now she, too, had a husband.

THE FLAMING SHIP OF OCRACOKE

After her true sex was revealed and accepted as Anne's had been, Mary and her bridegroom were allowed to sign on with Rackham's crew and put to sea with the promise of equal shares in any loot. But trouble developed almost immediately. Another pirate, one of the most hated and feared of the crew, promptly picked a quarrel with the new husband. A challenge to a duel to the death was quickly made and accepted. The alternative would have been a slit throat, but the prospect of the duel itself offered little more hope. Poor Mary! She knew full well that her new mate was no match for the other pirate and would probably be killed in the first passage at arms. If she had no husband, Calico Jack Rackham would probably not want her aboard; her entire piratical career was hanging in the balance.

With characteristic directness, Mary Read confronted her problem. Seeking out the challenging pirate, she demanded words with him. Smirking at what he thought would be her frantic pleas for her husband's life and hurriedly calculating what profit he could make out of the situation, the bully agreed to the conference. How confused he must have been when the first thing the woman did was to smack him with her open palm across his bearded face with all her considerable strength. Completely surprised and half blinded by the unexpected blow, the unsuspecting brigand struck back with his fist and, thus, sealed his own doom. Claiming mortal insult, Mary Read challenged him to a duel. Under the rules that governed such affairs at the time, she had the choice of the time and the place for the duel. Now smiling self-confidently, she chose the beach of a nearby island as the place. And the time? She named the time as exactly two hours before the scheduled duel between her husband and that same pirate.

For weapons, the unfortunate brigand chose both swords and pistols in close combat. But his fate was already decided, and he knew it. To his credit be it said that he put up a good fight for a few minutes before Mary Read's skill prevailed. She allowed him the one shot from his pistol, which missed. Then she proceeded to cut him to ribbons before she finally killed him. She wanted to set an example that other would-be challengers of her husband would remember, and she succeeded. Calico Jack sent a burial party ashore, and that was that.

Never again was the set-up challenged, and the reputation of the two married couples mushroomed. The very unnaturalness of the situation sent chills of horror down the spine of many an honest seafarer. Tales of the cruelty and complete lack of pity evidenced by the two women were exaggerated and multiplied time and again. Rumor fed on rumor until the two women were thought to be very fiends of hell itself. This pleased them no end, as it was exactly the impression they wished most to convey.

No matter what their other vices, the two women are said never to have indulged in strong drink, either ashore or afloat. It would have been better for them all if the other pirates had been abstainers too. At least they might have escaped capture longer. As it turned out, a British man-of-war, sent out from Jamaica to look for this very pirate ship, finally located the marauder lying at anchor off a beautiful little Caribbean island. Most of her pirate crew were roaring drunk below decks with only Anne, Mary, and two or three others on deck.

THE FLAMING SHIP OF OCRACOKE

The Britisher came alongside before the pirate could get her anchors up. Grappling irons were thrown over the rail, and a boarding party of British Marines swarmed aboard. Even then the buccaneers might have turned the tide if they had fought back. They heavily outnumbered their attackers and were as skilled in such fighting, but they were in no condition to fight, from Rackham on down. The sound of battle on the decks over their heads struck terror to their drunken brains, and they cowered below in fright as the tide of battle turned against those on deck. This so enraged Anne Bonny that she ran to an open hatchway, cursed them all for cowardly dogs, and then fired both her pistols into the hold, severely wounding several of her shipmates. All hands were either killed or quickly captured, and the two women were overpowered and put in leg irons. At the time of their capture, both Anne and Mary were wearing their attack clothes—huge, baggy trousers and heavy, mannish blouses with scarfs tied about their heads. Their captors did not suspect their sex, and the women did not reveal it to them.

The British Chief Magistrate, having been sent over from England only recently, did not suspect their true sex either, and no one seems to have informed His Honor. Anne Bonny and Mary Read maintained their disguise throughout the entire trial in Port Royal.

When the trial reached its predictable conclusion and Calico Jack Rackham was sentenced to be hanged in chains, His Majesty's chief legal officer in the islands turned his bewigged head to the others standing huddled in the well of the court. With a sarcastic edge to his voice, he asked if any of the others had anything to say concerning the question of whether they, also, should not be awarded a similar fate.

His Honor's eyebrows went up almost into his wig and his mouth dropped open in consternation as he beheld the youthful figures of two young pirates stride impertinently forward to address him.

"What possible reason could you two young scoundrels have to offer this Court as to why you should not be hanged by the neck until you are dead?" roared the Chief Magistrate.

Matching the judicial officer stare for stare and scowl for scowl, Anne Bonny tossed her head defiantly and replied, "Yer Majesty, we pleads our bellies!"

The shout of raucous laughter that went up from the pirates fairly made the rafters ring. Here was raw courage in the face of certain doom and a broad joke to end it all with. This the brigands could appreciate, and each identified himself at that moment with the defiant Anne. This was the rabbit spitting in the hound dog's face.

His Lordship turned white with anger. Pointing a trembling finger at the two lonely figures standing before him, he asked, "What is the meaning of this impertinence? Have you no fear of the hereafter?"

"Right is right, Yer Majesty," replied Anne. "Ye knows the English law as good or gooder than we does. Ye knows it's against the law to kill an unborned child and an English child at that. We both be pregnant, and ye cannot hang us."

Examination proved her to be right. Both Anne Bonny Rackham and Mary Read were in a family way and, under English law, could not be executed until after the birth of their children. But the other pirates had no such excuse and were not to escape.

A few days before Calico Jack's execution, Anne was allowed to visit him in his cell. Far from offering any condolences or consolation, Anne viewed her husband with contempt. "If ye had only fought like a man when the Britishers boarded us," she said, "ye might have died like a man instead of being hanged like a dog!" With that, she turned and flounced out of the cell. It was the last time she ever saw him.

Some time later, on the appointed day, Calico Jack Rackham, dressed in his bright and colorful calico trousers, was hanged in chains at high noon in the public square of Port Royal. His male crewmen were similarly dispatched a few minutes later, not only as a punishment for their crimes, but as a deterrent to others who might be tempted to go a-pirating.

Unlike Anne, Mary Read pleaded for her husband both at and after the trial. Swearing that the two of them had intended to forsake a life of piracy and settle down ashore, she begged for clemency, but in vain. It did her no good to plead that she herself was responsible for forcing her husband into piracy and that he had had no choice in the matter. He was hanged with the rest of them.

Mary contracted a fever soon after this and died in prison, attended to the end by Anne Bonny. Her child was never born. Mary's remains rest to this day in the beautiful little cemetery in Port Royal, where the soft trade winds blow over her grave and the tropic sun she loved so much shines down with a languorous warmth. She is remembered as "poor Mary Read" by the islanders.

True to her colors to the end, she is said to have remarked shortly before her death that it was good that the penalty for piracy was death by the gallows. "Otherwise," she said, "every cowardly milksop from here to hell might be led to try to belong to the Brotherhood of the Sea, since there would be no real penalty."

Anne Bonny was never hanged so far as is known. Transferred to the gaol in New Berne in the Province of Carolina, she was delivered of her child in safety. Through the influence of her father's friends, she received stay after stay of execution and was allowed to keep her baby in the gaol with her. Finally, she was pardoned altogether and left the New Berne gaol a free woman.

What happened to her after that is anyone's guess. Did she give away her red-headed baby boy and go back to sea to resume her piratical ways? Did she settle down in coastal Carolina and end her days as a midwife or a charwoman? Did she ever inherit any of her father's considerable wealth, or was it all used up in buying her pardon?

These and many more such questions will probably remain forever unanswered. Anne Bonny fades from sight with her release from prison and her pardon from the King. Perhaps she found peace and some degree of happiness in her old age. Perhaps, just perhaps, that beautiful, young, raven-haired girl you saw helping her father with his shrimp trawl in Core Sound has the blood of Anne Bonny in her veins. It is entirely possible.

The Legend Writ on Rocke

In September, 1937, an out-of-state tourist named L. E. Hammond was traveling by automobile through the eastern plains of North Carolina. This was a pleasure trip, and having no hard and fast schedule to abide by, Hammond was taking his time and enjoying the scenery. He approached Edenton from the westward over the newly built causeway and earth fill, which connects the town with the concrete bridge over the four-mile-wide Chowan River. A complete wilderness surrounded him on every side, and he became engrossed with its natural beauty. As he traversed the raised highway through the swampy low grounds of the Chowan, he spied what he took to be the fall foliage of a large number of hickory trees, growing fairly close to the road on relatively dry ground.

According to the story the tourist told later, not only was he fond of hickory nuts, but he was also in need of a break, for he had been driving many hours without relief. Now in those days there were not as many filling stations and rest areas along the highways as there are today, so Hammond parked his car on the broad shoulder of the highway and walked into the woods until he was sure he was out of sight of the road. He had gone something less than a quarter of a mile when he stumbled and fell headlong over a stone protruding from the ground. After arising and kicking the stone, he examined it with more care and found it to be roughly oval in shape with strange writing carved into its surface.

Intrigued, Hammond lugged the thirty-pound stone to the nearby river and washed the mud, muck, and trash from its face. The carvings remained; the words and symbols seemed to have been roughly chiseled by hand into the stone, but he could not make heads or tails of them.

The traveler had heard several legends about the pirate Blackbeard. He had also heard many times that the bulk of the old brigand's treasure had never been found and that the pirate had boasted that only he and the devil knew where it was buried. Hammond knew, too, that Blackbeard had sailed the nearby waters and had even maintained a large home near Edenton. Could it be, he wondered, that this virgin forest so near the broad Chowan River contained the hiding place of that treasure? And was this a pirate message crudely chiseled in stone in an unintelligible language to hide its secret from the casual observer?

He had heard of such things, and a strong case of treasure fever took hold of him. The antiquity of the carvings seemed obvious to him, and the inscription was certainly mysterious. Looking carefully all around to see if he had been observed, Hammond, with great haste and some furtiveness, carried the stone back to his automobile, locked it safely in the trunk, and drove off with it.

Shades of Long John Silver! A pirate's message carved in stone! Well, the countryside was wild enough looking for it. The forest was extremely dense and seemingly virgin. Many huge cypress trees, which looked to be hundreds of years old, grew there, and the paved highway had only recently been cut through the unspoiled wilderness. It could be. It just could be. At any rate, the tourist wasn't about to show his find to anyone in the Edenton area. If there was to be a pirate treasure, he wanted it all for himself. And so he took the mysterious stone away from the area where it was discovered.

According to his story, Hammond carried the stone in the trunk of his car wherever he went, and he tried to get the writing deciphered in several states other than North Carolina. But, try as he might, no one could throw any light on it for him. He was still looking for the hidden meaning, the treasure clues he felt must be there, when, in November of that same year, he happened to be in Atlanta, Georgia. He took the time to visit some friends there, and over cocktails that night, he told them of his find and of his growing despair of ever discovering the message. He even led them out to his car and showed the mysterious stone to them.

Upon his friends' urging, Hammond took the stone to Emory University in Atlanta the next day, where he met a Dr. Haywood Pearce, a professor of American history. With some difficulty, Dr. Pearce, with the aid of other faculty members, deciphered the message.

On the face of the stone was carved a Latin cross and below this cross was chiseled:

> ANNANIAS DARE &
> VIRGINIA WENT HENCE
> VNTO HEAVEN 1591
> ANYE ENGLISHMAN SHEW
> JOHN WHITE, GOVR VIA

On the reverse side of the stone, the following message had been laboriously and crudely inscribed:

FATHER SOONE AFTER YOV GOE FOR
    ENGLAND WE CAM HITHER
ONLIE MISARIE & WARRE TOW YEARE
ABOVE HALFE DEADE ERE TOW YEARE
MORE FROM SICKNESS
BEINE FOVRE AND TWENTIE
SALVAGE WITH MESSAGE OF SHIP VNTO VS

THE FLAMING SHIP OF OCRACOKE

SMAL SPACE OF THIME THEY AFFRITE OF
    REVENGE
RANN AL AWAYE
WE BELIEVE IT NOTT YOV
SOON AFTER YE SALVAGES FAINE SPIRITS
    ANGRIE
SVDDAINE MVRTHER AL SAVE SEAVEN
MINE CHILD—ANNANIAS TO SLAINE WITH
    MVCH MISARIE
BVRIE AL NEERE FOVRE EASTE THIS RIVER
    VPON SMAL HIL
NAMES ALL WRIT THERE ON ROCKE
PVTT THIS THER ALSOE
SALVAGE SHEW THIS VNTO YOV & HITHER
    WEE PROMISE
YOV TO GIVE GREAT PLENTIE PRESENTS
        E W D

The stone appeared to be a message to John White, the governor of Raleigh's Lost Colony, from his daughter Eleanor White Dare. It began to dawn on Hammond that, although the stone had nothing whatever to do with pirate treasure, it might be of immense value as a historic relic.

In 1587, Governor White had set sail for England for supplies, and he planned a prompt return. When he sailed from Roanoke Island, he left behind some eighty-nine men, seventeen women, nine boys, and two infants, including his own daughter Eleanor, her husband Ananias Dare, and their infant daughter Virginia. For days the colonists had urged his departure so that he might the sooner return with the needed provisions. Governor White had

tarried long enough to see his granddaughter safely born
and formally baptized. When he left, the little band was
in good shape, the Indians were friendly, and prospects
seemed bright.

But England's preoccupation with the Spanish Armada
delayed his return trip, for Queen Elizabeth could not
and would not spare ships and seamen for a voyage to the
colonies when the very life of the kingdom was threat-
ened. Governor White's supply ships were needed for the
impending naval battle, and his sailors were required to
defend England herself.

When the Armada was soundly defeated and practically destroyed, Governor White was permitted to return
to the colony. Landing on Roanoke Island on August 18,
1590, his granddaughter's third birthday, he found the
settlement abandoned. The distraught old man searched
as best he could for the colonists until severe autumn
storms forced the return of his ships to England. He never
saw Eleanor or Virginia again, and with his departure,
the best chance for recovery of the missing colony was
lost forever.

The mystery of the Lost Colony has remained one of
the most fascinating riddles of American history. Many
are the legends that surround the tale, but nothing is
known that amounts to actual historical proof. Thus,
Hammond's stone created great excitement at Emory
University when it was thought that the message carved
on it was possibly the first real clue to the disappearance of
Raleigh's colonists.

Examination by the university's geology department
revealed the stone to be a piece of rough veined quartz,

and the moss on its surface was classified as being very old. The stone had not been quarried but had apparently crumbled off some ancient outcropping, and the edges were still very rough.

Dr. Pearce, with financing from the university, returned with Hammond to the scene near Edenton where the stone had been found. According to the carving, there had been "fovre and twentie" in the little band, and of that number, "al save seaven" had been murdered. This left seventeen "names all writ there on rocke," and it was this list, plus the graves of those murdered colonists, that the expedition hoped to find.

The party made a thorough search of the surrounding area, but they found no more carved stones of any sort. Laying out a circle eight miles in diameter, they meticulously combed the ground for the "smal hil" mentioned in the carving, but they saw no such hill. The searchers did not attempt to uproot trees or undertake any extensive removal of the surface soil. This would have been tremendously difficult, as the forest was, and is to this day, extremely dense.

Upon their return to Atlanta, Dr. Pearce and Mr. Hammond finally decided to give their story to the newspapers. The *Atlanta Journal* did a special feature on the stone, as did many other southern newspapers. The stories all carried the information that the university would gladly pay a reasonable sum for any similar stones which carried inscriptions that could be tied in with the first stone.

Immediately the university began to receive numerous calls from people with unusual stones. Most of these stones proved to be either so badly eroded as to be illegible or very old grave markers. Finally, however, a man named William Eberhart came in with a stone he had found embedded in a small hill on the banks of a river about twelve miles south of Greenville, South Carolina. Eberhart, a stonemason, frequently searched for stones lying about on river banks and in wilderness places, since he could have such stones for no cost and could use them in his work. Eberhart had gone no farther in school than the third grade and could neither read nor write, but he had kept this particular stone as a sort of good luck piece, since it contained what he called "Indian writings" on both sides.

Like the Edenton stone, this one was covered with ancient moss and was crudely carved on both sides and the edge with inscriptions in Elizabethan English. The face of the stone read:

HEYR LAETH ANANIAS & VIRGINIA
FATHER SALVAGE MVRTHER AL SAVE
   SEAVEN
NAMES WRITTEN HEYR
MAI GOD HAB MERCYE
ELEANOR DARE 1591

The edge of the stone was inscribed with the words: FATHER WEE GOE SW. A list of fifteen names was chiseled on the reverse. The names were SYDNOR, BOANE, WIGAN, BIRGE, POLLE, CAREWE, BOWMAN, SPRAGUE, TUCKERS, BOLITOE, SMYTHE, SAKERS, HOLBORN, WINGET, and STOATE. Together with Ananias and Virginia, these fifteen made up the murdered seventeen!

Eberhart took Dr. Pearce to the small hill where he

had found the stones, and Dr. Pearce actually bought the land. An extensive search began on and around the hill, and several more stones were found.

Many months later, various hunters and fishermen reported new finds in a remote area near Gainesville, Georgia. A total of nine stones were found and turned over to Dr. Pearce. Still later, twenty-two stones were discovered up and down the banks of the Chattahoochee River in the general vicinity of Atlanta. The location of the last twenty-two stones had long been known to anthropologists as the site of a large Cherokee Indian town for hundreds of years.

Obviously, the stones were not found in chronological order, but many of them were dated, and when arranged in what seems to be a logical sequence, they told a broken, intriguing narrative of Eleanor Dare's years of wandering with an Indian tribe and her final settlement in a large, southern village, where she married the chief and bore him a daughter.

> FATHER WEE GOE SW WITH FOVRE GOODLIE
> MEN
> THEY SHEW MOCHE MERCYE
> THEY ARE GOOD SOVLDIOVRS
> THEY SAIDE THEY BROWT VS TOW YOV
> ELEANOR DARE 1591

This one dated 1595 tells of Eleanor Dare's marriage:

> FATHER SHEW MOCHE MERCYE TOW
> GREATE SALVAGE LODGEMENT
> THEIR KING HAB MEE TOW WIFE
> SITHENCE 1592

The Legend Writ on Rocke

The tale unfolds further in these two messages:

> FATHER I HAB DOWTER HEYR
> ALL SAVE SALVAGE KING ANGRIE
> ELEANOR DARE 1595

> FATHER SOME AMANGE VS PVTT
> MANYE MESSAGE FOR YOV BYE TRAILE
> FATHER I BESEECHE YOV
> HAV MYE DOWTER GOE TO ENGLANDE
> (1598)

And this pitiful message was the last dated one to be signed in the name of Eleanor Dare:

> FATHER I HAB MOCHE
> SVDDAINE SICKNESS
> ELEANOR DARE 1599

The very last stone of all is signed with neither the name nor the initials of Eleanor Dare. It bears the name of Griffin Jones, one of the colonists. One wonders if it might have been he who laboriously chiseled all the messages over the years. The last stone, also dated 1599, reads:

> SHEW [J]OHN WHITE ELEANOR DYE
> FEBRVARY
> DOWTER NAME AGNES HEYR

Thus ends the legend that was "writ on rocke."

The suggestion has been advanced that the entire rock diary was an ingenious, elaborate hoax. Still, some believe that the stones are a historical record of the fate of the Lost Colony. It is not the author's intention to attempt either to prove or disprove the validity of the stones.

Edenton, where the first stone was found, was once the site of the Indian town of Weapomeoc, or Meeting-of-the-Waters, and Raleigh's colonists must have known of its existence, even though it is some fifty miles into the mainland from Roanoke Island. Even before the Lost Colony left England, Sir Ralph Lane had visited Weapomeoc and had reported concerning the settlement to Queen Elizabeth and Raleigh. But it is a long, long way from Edenton to Atlanta. However, Chief Manteo, who was known to the colonists, was a chief of the Matchapungo Tribe, a member of the Cherokee Nation, whose lands stretched from southern Georgia into Virginia.

It is interesting to speculate, to see if the pieces can be fitted together in this, one of history's greatest puzzles. There is something appealing in the legend of a lonely, frightened English woman being held captive by Indians, seeing her husband and daughter murdered, traveling the long miles by foot and canoe from one end of the Cherokee Nation to the other, and finally being accepted by the tribe.

But, as it is with so many of the Lost Colony legends, no one can be sure that the stones tell the truth. It is doubtful if anyone will ever know.

Freshponds Will

There are many tales about the naming of Kill Devil Hill.
It was to this hill that the Wright Brothers came, searching
for a steady, dependable air current, and it was very near
this same hill that they successfully undertook the first

powered flight in a heavier-than-air craft. But the hill, now crowned with a huge granite pylon and stabilized by turf, was given its name long before Orville and Wilbur Wright were born.

The most recent account of the name's origin has to do with an enterprising gentleman who, it is said, operated an illicit whiskey still in the woods that lie west of the large sand dune. His complete disregard for anything like quality control, plus the fact that alert revenue agents kept him constantly moving his still from one thicket to another, resulted in an end product that was infamous over the entire coastal region. The liquor, which he sold in fruit jars, was nauseous to the smell and taste and produced hangovers of gargantuan and near-fatal intensity. But if one got the stuff down and made it stay, the results were immediate and euphoric. That is, until one woke up to the most exquisite and disabling physical illness this side of Hell. The whiskey was so bad that it was generally acknowledged to be bad enough to "kill the Devil." Thus the hill where it was obtainable was known as Kill Devil Hill.

Another legend tells of Devil Ike, a man so huge that he towered head and shoulders over his companions and so fearless that it was said he feared no one, not even the Devil. He was hired by an insurance representative to guard the cargo of a beached ship. The cargo was to be shipped to Norfolk instead of being sold at "vendee," or wreck-auction, where such cargoes went for ridiculously low prices. At such auctions, the natives usually benefited because only they lived near enough to justify transportation of the goods to the point of ultimate use.

The Outer Bankers, having rescued crew and cargo from the sea, assumed that they would be able to bid on the cargo at the vendee, and when it was found that no vendee would be held, they were very much upset. To their mind, the owners and the insurance company were "stealing" the cargo from them.

Thereafter, portions of the cargo began to just disappear every night, although native guards were hired to protect it. These caretakers, professing ignorance of the missing property, opined that the Devil himself must be making off with it piecemeal. Thus, Devil Ike, himself a dyed-in-the-wool Outer Banker, was hired in hopes that he could save the dwindling cargo.

The very first night, as he rested shortly after midnight, his blunderbuss by his side, Devil Ike saw something that made even his blood run cold. Part of the cargo, a bale of silk, began to move suddenly and without apparent cause.

Crouching low, Devil Ike ran to intercept the moving bale. Rounding a small hillock, he encountered a lifelong friend astride a sturdy marsh pony, which was straining to pull a rope the other end of which was tied to the traveling bale of silk. This, then, was the secret of the dwindling cargo. It was being hauled off, piece by piece, by the disgruntled fishermen who thought themselves cheated of their just and ancient rights.

Now the fearless guard was faced with a difficult choice. He could turn informer and be branded as a traitor by his friends and neighbors. Or he could forget the whole matter and become an accomplice in the crime.

He solved his problem in the simple, direct way of the Outer Banker. After warning his friend that any repetition of the thievery would bring instant disclosure and probable prosecution, Devil Ike burned the rope in two with one blast from his blunderbuss, sending the frightened pony scampering into the woods, its owner clinging wildly to the reins.

From that day forward, the thefts stopped and Devil Ike boasted to all that he had killed the Devil, who had been stealing the cargo. And from that time on, the huge dune where this took place was known as Kill Devil Hill.

The old-timers scoff at both these stories. They say that the "real" story has to do with a man who is known in history only as Freshponds Will. It seems that Will was an actual person who was known to the British authorities. At any rate, the British Colonial Census, taken back before the death of Blackbeard in 1718, makes mention of him. He was identified as a hermit who lived in a cave dug into a sand bank near the Fresh Ponds, those two elliptical lakes that provide fresh water for the Bankers, and subsisted by trapping, hunting, and fishing. Though the Colonial Records do not indicate that he owned anything worth being taxed by the Crown, they do list him as a loyal subject.

The life of a hermit on the Outer Banks, while it sounds romantic and carefree, can become an existence of semi-hunger and frequent discomfort, even to one hardened to life in the wild. And so it was with Will. He was skillful and energetic enough to keep himself supplied with foods and skins, but he longed for an easier life. In fact, he became so fed up with his lot that he resolved to seek out the aid of the Devil.

Now, Will had no idea how to communicate with His

Satanic Majesty, but he knew a witch in Nag's Head Woods who should know.

"Certainly," she told him when he sought her aid, "there is a tried and true method by which the Devil may be evoked, but take care that you do not call him for nothing. There is a strict protocol that must be observed, though, and one must perform the requisite incantations in just the right manner."

Of course, these incantations were known only to practicing witches and were available for a price. "After all, good sir," the witch continued, "witches and warlocks have to live, too, and all an honest witch has to sell is her knowledge, her training, and her professional services."

After some bargaining on the part of the hermit, and not a little haggling on the part of the witch, a price was agreed upon, and Will duly paid her three prime fox skins, six rabbit skins, and the hide of a muskrat in return for detailed instructions on the proven and tested method for evoking Satan. Will repeated it over and over again until it became fixed in his memory.

Filled with excitement and eager to try his newly acquired education, the hermit found a sand dune not too far from his Fresh Ponds that met the requirement of being higher than ninety but less than one hundred feet. Having found the suitable locale, Will waited impatiently for the dark of the moon to roll around. When at last the date was right, he went to the hill. He was loaded down with the paraphernalia the witch had assured him was necessary.

Old Will must have learned his lesson well, for after having gone through the incantations only nine times, he suddenly was confronted with the Devil himself. There he stood—urbane, handsome, smiling, but deadly and menacing as well. It is stated, on best authority of folk memory, that Satan's first utterance on that occasion, an extended and inquisitive "Well–l–l–l?" sounded exactly like a long roll of thunder.

It is certain that Will's knees shook violently and that his whole body trembled with fear. Only the extreme weakness he suddenly experienced in his lower legs prevented his headlong flight down the steep side of that sand dune and back to the relative safety of his cave. Then as now, however, the Devil had his ways of putting people at ease and gaining their confidence. It was not many minutes before he and Freshponds Will were seated on the very top of that sand hill, conversing as freely and familiarly as though they had known each other for years. Will's discontent with his station in life and his willingness to go to nearly any length to improve his lot fell on eagerly receptive ears, and a bargain was soon struck.

The party of the first part was to give to Freshponds Will a leather bag filled with gold coins. No ordinary leather bag, mind you, and no ordinary gold coins, but a pouch that would refill itself each and every night, no matter how much was spent out of it by day, with brand-new, gleaming gold crowns. In return, our hermit was to deed over to the Devil his immortal soul. It was agreed that Satan, in turn, would mark Will's forehead with the brand of Hell. All this was in token of the bargain that Will's soul, upon his death, should forever belong to Satan.

But not that night! The agreement was made that night,

but it would take a little time to prepare the pouch and set up the supply of gold pieces. So the contractors agreed to meet again in one lunar month on that same ninety-one-foot hill when, once again, the scene would be veiled in darkness.

Stumbling through the blackness on his way back to his cave, Will was filled with exultation over the bargain he had made. Riches, great riches, would be his for all his life! For the rest of his mortal days, no matter how much he spent, his bag of gold would always be replenished and ready for more spending, more buying, more possessing of the good things of life. Fine foods would be his for the buying. Fine clothes would replace his garb of animal skins, and a splendid home would replace his often damp, mosquito-infested cave. Men would envy him, and beautiful women would admire him. He would be the most sought-after person in his entire generation!

For *all* his life? Now Will stopped in his tracks, and his body trembled as he contemplated the bargain he had made. Plodding on to his cave, he began to have serious second thoughts about who had received the better end of the bargain.

In his troubled dreams that night, the image of his beloved, but long dead, mother floated before him with a reproachful and sorrowing look upon her lovely face. She had always taught him to live an upright and honest life, fearing God and loving Him and trying his best to conduct himself in such a manner as to receive the reward promised to those who persevere in their quest for true righteousness. And now he had deliberately thrown all this away! He had, indeed, made a devil's bargain with the Devil. He had not the slightest doubt but that Satan would hold him to the letter of his agreement and exact full payment.

The hermit could think of nothing else all the next day. It did not help matters that a rainy northeaster had set in, and everything about his cave was damp and clammy. Freshponds Will had, indeed, hit bottom in his feelings of despair and loneliness. It had been bad enough before, but now he had the prospect of eternal damnation to consider.

About midday, Will set out with his leather bucket to get drinking water from the nearby Fresh Ponds. Still preoccupied with his dilemma, he was not as careful as usual in picking his route. He normally threaded his way with care because then, as now, the vicinity was pretty well populated with venomous snakes. But, today, he veered off the trail and suddenly found himself mired to his knees in a little puddle of sand, which had been made soft and slushy by the rain. With some difficulty, he extricated his legs from the sinkhole, but, in so doing, he lost one of his moccasins. At that very instant, Will had a flash of inspiration. He saw a possible way out of his plight.

"Ho," he shouted at the top of his lungs, dancing about with one foot shod and the other bare. "Ho, that will do it! That will save my immortal soul and still let me outwit the Devil. If only I can bring it off! If only he does not suspect!"

Nightfall found Will back on the summit of the high hill on which he had met the Devil. A stout spade and a large wicker basket were in his hands, and the fire of hope and determination was in his eyes. All night long Will dug down into the very heart of that hill, filling his basket with sand and then dragging the filled basket to be dumped at the westerly base of the hill. Deeper and ever deeper he dug the shaft, straight down, in spite of heart-breaking cave-ins and sand slides which constantly hampered his work.

As the first hints of gray began to lighten the sky over the ocean, Will picked up his tools and hurried back to his cave, where he soon fell into the deep sleep of utter exhaustion.

Each night that followed, except for those hours during which a full moon spread its muted brilliance over the scene, Will was back at his hill digging. His shaft was becoming so deep that he had to fashion crude ladders in order to drag his loaded basket to the shaft opening. Some shoring on the sides was necessary, too, and the hermit had to spend valuable time looking for boards which would serve this purpose.

Deeper and deeper sank the bottom of the hole under Will's frenzied efforts until he was positive he was approaching the very base of the hill. Surely the shaft was almost as deep as the hill was tall, and Will would soon know whether the old legends about the foundations of these hills were true, as he believed them to be.

Then, on the 26th night, it happened! Thrusting his spade deep into the sand floor of the shaft, Freshponds Will found himself unable to withdraw it. Slowly the spade sank into the sand until the handle disappeared with a little, wet gurgle. Not only that, but the bottom of Will's crude ladder began to disappear more and more rapidly into the sand, and before he knew it, his legs had sunk to the knees as he felt the powerful suction of quicksand. The legend was true! Quicksand was at the base of his hill!

Struggling frantically, Will was just barely able to free himself and climb back up the shaft, even as the bottom of the hole ballooned slightly and the floor of his excavation liquified and took on the true characteristics of deadly quicksand. The topmost rungs of the trapped ladder disappeared under the watery surface with a sinister slurp, as Will listened from the top of the sand dune.

Happy that his toil was almost done, the hermit hummed to himself as he went about the wooded area below the hill gathering great armloads of dried and rotten branches with which he carefully covered the opening he had made at the top of the dune. Once the mouth of the pit was covered, it took only a few minutes to sprinkle dry sand over the branches and leaves. The trap was completely hidden.

Back at his cave, Will once again slept the sleep of exhaustion, but, this time, with only happy dreams. Once again the face of his mother played a prominent part, but this time she smiled and looked at him with an air of fervent hope as if she, too, desired that his plan succeed.

The trap was set, and the time for the attempt was at hand. As the hour of midnight on the twenty-eighth night approached, Freshponds Will was already at the rendezvous. The night was as black as the Devil's heart, and a half gale was whining through the sea oats with a mournful, foreboding sound. Off to the southwest a grumble of thunder persisted and reverberated. A bone-chilling drizzle began to fall. It was a pitch-black night, a night fit for evil. No star shone and no hearth light from any habitation pierced the gloom. It was a time for shipwreck and murder and treachery. It was a night for all sensible people to stay snug at home.

Not for the Fresh Ponds hermit, though. This was his "do or die" night. This was his effort and his only chance, so he thought, to save his immortal soul from eternal damnation, and he was determined to see it through. There, on the crest of the ninety-one-foot sand hill, Will waited and watched and strained every muscle and nerve as he sought the first indication of Satan's arrival.

He did not have long to wait. The Devil was never one to keep a prospect waiting, and this night was no exception. As the witching hour arrived, a strange, almost phosphorescent glow became evident in the sea. It grew brighter by the minute until the whole depth of the ocean appeared to be afire with this strange light. Turbulence developed around the focal point of the glow, until the surface was not only lighted, but stirred into a very maelstrom.

Out of the troubled sea, this vortex of unnatural light and motion, the Devil appeared. Swiftly, but with a firm and measured tread, as if he listened to the cadence of some mighty symphony, Satan strode up the beach and directly to the foot of the huge dune. On he marched, up the first easy slope of the hill, as Freshponds Will stood, erect and motionless, at the very top and just to the westward of his disguised trap.

As the Devil approached, Will could see a beautiful chamois leather pouch in his left hand and, in his right, a white-hot branding iron bearing the number 666, the Devil's own brand, his sign of ownership. Will feigned a frenzy of desire for the pouch of gold pieces. He danced and leaped about, holding out his right hand to the Devil in a begging gesture, but being very sure to stay just to the west of the camouflaged mouth of the deep shaft.

"Throw it to me, Sire," yelled Will. "Throw me my bag of gold and then come and place your mark upon my forehead. I must feel your gold before you claim my soul. I must see your gold before I yield my soul."

Strangely, and with a satanic smile of indulgence, the Devil did just what the hermit asked him to do. As he approached within ten or fifteen feet, he tossed the bag directly to Will. Then he raised the glowing branding iron, much after the manner in which an expert whaler raises his harpoon, and, grinning evilly, he ran straight for his intended victim. On he rushed, out over the mouth of the trap. Then down, down, down into the shaft Will had dug, screaming with rage and frustration as he fell.

The hermit heard the sizzle as the watery sand engulfed the hot iron. He heard Satan's scream cut off abruptly as his mouth filled with the slimy quicksand, and then, after a large sulphuric bubble or two, there was silence. You see, Will had stumbled upon another ancient fact. The Devil has no power over quicksand.

"Free," screamed Will into the teeth of the whining wind. "Free, and saving my immortal soul." Then, as the enormity of what he had done dawned on him, he began a kind of war dance around and around the hole as he kicked more and more sand into the crumbling shaft. "I've killed the Devil," he shouted. "I've killed the old Devil; I've killed the Devil."

And this, old-timers claim, is really how Kill Devil Hill

got its name. It is certain that the name appears on some of the very oldest maps of the region. Most of the oldest settlers, the permanent people, believe this yarn.

Did Freshponds Will really kill the Devil? Is the Devil still trapped in the quicksand that lies at the foundation of Kill Devil Hill? Some people say that, on any dark and moonless night, the screams of the imprisoned Devil can still be heard. Others point to the evil rampant upon the earth today and say that Satan, sandfiddler like, found an escape route out of his prison.

Let us hope this is not so.

Porpoise Sal

*Just across Back Sound from Harker's Island lies a por-*tion of the Outer Banks called Shackleford Banks. Largely deserted now, this beautiful coastal island once contained one of the largest settlements on the entire coast. It was called Diamond City, and its population is said to have numbered several hundred permanent residents.

In the middle eighteen hundreds, this thriving community was the location of a very productive whaling industry, as well as a porpoise fishery. Both whales and porpoises were sought for the oil that was produced, or rendered, from their carcasses, and both were caught by a shore-based operation that involved putting out to sea in small boats for the capture. As can well be imagined, this tended to produce seamanship and courage of the highest order. Whale and porpoise capture, plus fishing for food, provided an ample income for the residents. Thrifty as well as hardy, they supplemented their seafood diet by the produce from their fertile gardens. Any man worth his salt could live very pleasantly in those days if he but half applied himself. It was a good life and a healthy one. The large percentage of very old people was proof of that.

This seaside Garden of Eden flourished until the month of August in 1899, when fate brought a dramatic and more or less abrupt end to this happy way of life. At that time, one of the worst coastal storms in all of recorded history struck the little island with devastating gales. So awesome was the brute force of the wind that the angry surf actually broke all the way across the island and into Back Sound on the north. Many of the houses were washed from their foundations by the storm, and some of the residents took shelter on the rooftops to escape drowning. Others watched from their second-story bedrooms as the water rose relentlessly up and up the staircase until the whole first floor was flooded to the ceiling. A number of the homes actually floated free like huge, ungainly ships driven before the wind until they fetched up against some of the trees then growing on the island and thus were saved from complete destruction. It was a natural disaster of such magnitude that it lingers to this day in the folk memory of those Bankers.

The storm finally wore itself out, and the waters subsided, leaving Diamond City littered with wreckage. Spars and barnacle-covered timbers from old, wrecked ships, parts of roofs, and the shattered lumber from destroyed houses lay all over the beach. It was a wild and desolate scene, mute testimony to the storm's fury.

Amidst all the torn and twisted debris lay a beautiful young woman, securely tied to what appeared to be the hatch cover from a ship. Covered with ugly bruises, she seemed to be half drowned, but she was still breathing very faintly. She made feeble, struggling movements, as though to free herself from the bowline and half-hitch knots that secured her to the hatch cover. The islanders had never seen her or anyone like her before. That she could have lived through that storm tied to a hatch cover was hard to believe. Hard to believe, that is, if she were really human.

The women of the community forgot themselves and their own losses in their spontaneous and eager efforts to help this stranger, for she was a being in worse plight than themselves. Making haste to give her aid and comfort, they put together a makeshift bed in one of the least-damaged houses and employed time-proven folk remedies to bring about her return to consciousness. Consciousness, yes, but normalcy, no. From the moment of her recovery, the sea waif was never in what the Bankers considered to be her right mind.

Two things were noticed by the island women right away. One, the sea waif wore a plain gold wedding band on the ring finger of her left hand, and, two, she was very obviously pregnant. Supposition and conjecture ran rampant as these good women tried to guess her origin and her station in life. All they were ever really able to do was guess. Her beautiful green eyes wore that vacant, staring look so common to people who have undergone great shock. At first, she spoke in jumbles of unconnected words that made no sense at all. When asked her name, she would murmur over and over, "Sallie, Sallie, Sallie." Nothing else. She was a lovely, appealing derelict. Human or not, she desperately needed human help, and human love and sympathy.

Diamond City, or what was left of it, took Sallie to its heart. She repaid them with a lifetime of conduct so bizarre and mysterious as to provide them with a never-ending source of speculation, gossip, and wonder. She was never able to remember who she was or where she came from, but she spoke with a quiet, cultured voice, and her field of general knowledge seemed to be extensive. The island people truly believed that she had what they called second sight. They ascribed to her many powers that were both superhuman and awesome. There were times when it seemed they were exactly right in doing so.

From the beginning of her stay, Sal assured the Bankers that the terrible August storm had been a judgment upon them "for killing the poor porpoise people." Time and again she repeated, with a sorrowful shake of her head, what she said were the names of these betrayed porpoises. Diamond City people had thought all along that she was "off her rocker," and this kind of talk only served to confirm their suspicions. From then on, she was known as "Porpoise Sal" or, sometimes, "The Wrack Woman." She was treated with the deference and respect so often accorded, by many people, to the mentally afflicted. One "touched of God" was deemed to be especially dear to Him and thus deserving of especially tender and forbearing treatment.

It was said that she actually talked to porpoises. For many years, tales kept cropping up that she had been seen, waist-deep in the ocean, surrounded by several porpoises, which were not leaping and cavorting as they usually do but were lying very still in the water, breathing softly through their blowholes, and listening as she rubbed their bellies and talked to them. Proof? Of course there never was any, but the story kept popping up with amazing frequency and with an occasional change of locale.

In an earlier day or in a different locality, she might well have been burned as a witch. Diamond City residents, though, were tolerant, kindly people, who rather enjoyed the excitement of having such a creature in their midst. Besides, it was far wiser to stay on the good side of someone who might be in league with the awful powers of Mother Sea. And so Sal and the Bankers coexisted in an atmosphere of mutual respect not unmixed with sincere affection.

Of course, it was probably only coincidence that the porpoise fishery soon went out of business and that the whaling continued for only a few more years, but Diamond City was never really the same after that August storm. The very next year people began to move away, many of them to Harker's Island, where their descendants still live. Some of these people actually tore down their houses and moved them, piece by piece, over the sound to Harker's, where they put them back together again.

Porpoise Sal didn't move, though. She stayed on and watched Diamond City die, and she became part of the legend of the island. Soon after she was able to be up and about, she began to mumble disjointed sentences about having been promised a home, although she did not say by whom. She moved from house to house at the invitation of the kind Diamond City folk, but although she was made as welcome and as comfortable as possible on these visits, she never seemed to be happy and kept talking about the promised home which had not been forthcoming. It wasn't that she complained or that she was unappreciative of the hospitality shown her. She just expected a home of her own, and she made no secret of it.

Under the circumstances, it came as no great surprise to anyone that when, a few months later, a powerful storm blew up from the southwest and died away a few days later, there, down the beach a little ways, was an empty oak vat or hogshead. It was some ten feet in diameter and fully twenty feet long, with one end missing—nothing like any barrel the Bankers had ever seen before. Some thought it might have been used in curing leather, and others believed that perhaps it originated in some brewery. However, there was never a moment's doubt by anyone that the barrel was Porpoise Sal's long-expected home. It had come to her from the sea and was hers and hers alone.

THE FLAMING SHIP OF OCRACOKE

The fishermen banded together, rolled the big vat up beyond the reach of even a storm tide, and braced it as well as they could with stout timbers which they anchored in the sand. They fashioned a cap for the open end. Into this they cut a doorway and hung a solid wood door therein. The door faced to the west, toward Beaufort Inlet, since this was the direction of the prevailing summer breeze. They cut windows in the two sides and in the east end of the huge barrel. They laid a level floor of boards inside and built a bunk into the shoreward side. Then they brought a woodburning stove, secured its legs to the floor with staples, as in a ship's galley, and ran a stovepipe through the ceiling. Porpoise Sal had been given her own home at last through the whim of the sea and the generosity of the Bankers. Here she was to stay for years to come, fitting into the beach as naturally as a sandfiddler or a sea gull.

Sal's baby was born that winter with the assistance of both the local midwives, and a fine, strapping baby boy he was. She was hard put to decide on a name for him, and her neighbors suggested a wealth of fine old Biblical names like Ahab and Jonah and Obed, but none of their suggestions was to her liking. She gave her baby lots of love and sometimes spoke to him as though she were talking to another adult. On such occasions, she would always preface her remarks by saying in a loud, clear voice, "Now, mark you this!" So often was this done that the baby began to look up every time he heard the phrase. The neighbors immediately picked it up, and the little boy soon became known as "Mark You This." As time went on, this was shortened to just Mark or Sal's Mark.

Sal educated her son as best she could. She trained him to read and write a little and to do simple sums, but, above all, she impressed upon him the necessities of fearing God and doing right by his fellow man. In addition, Sal instilled in him her own love of the sea, the wind, and the stars. She taught him to sit perfectly still and listen for the message of the ocean as it talked its prophetic language. In her own way, she explained the intimate relationship of man with the sea and counseled him to respect and admire all the finny and shelled inhabitants of the cradle of all life.

Mark did not have an easy life as a child. His situation was a bit unusual, and children have a tendency to be cruel to others who are different from them in any way. But there were good times, too, when he and his mother went fishing or crabbing. And the boy never doubted that his mother loved him.

One spring, while Mark was still a little toddler, a sick whale died in the sea off Shackleford Banks, and a ball of ambergris as big as a man's head washed ashore directly in front of Sal's barrel house. Now ambergris is a substance formed in the internal organs of sperm whales, which they expel from their bodies in a way unknown to man. To the makers of fine perfumes, this substance is literally worth its weight in gold. Although very rare, it is a necessary ingredient of the world's finest and most expensive perfumes. So precious is the stuff that men have fought and died for the possession of it. And Sal was aware of its value. She saw it lying there in the wash, recognized it, scooped it up, and ran with it to her house, where she hid the treasure under her bunk.

Later that same day, the carcass of the whale washed

ashore a short distance down the beach, and a large crowd, excited by the possibility of great riches, gathered in search of ambergris.

Trustful Sal just could not keep her secret to herself. She told some of her nearest neighbors about her good fortune, and they, in turn, told others. The news spread like wildfire and it was soon a matter of common knowledge that the Wrack Woman had found ambergris and, most assuredly, must have it hidden in her shack. Most people were genuinely glad to hear of her good fortune, but she was also the recipient of several envious looks.

The next midnight two rough-looking outlanders, who had heard of the sea waif's find, kicked in her door. Holding a case knife to her throat, they demanded the ambergris. Sal was speechless with fright and shock and could only shake her head from side to side and look at the robbers with large, pleading eyes. She fully expected to have her throat slit if she did not reveal her treasure, but she was thinking clearly enough, even in her terror, to realize that she could expect no mercy once her assailants had the stuff in their hands.

As Little Mark slept unnoticed in his tiny trundle bed, the roughnecks dragged Sal outside and proceeded to kick loose the timbers that held her house in place. Then, straining and prying with all their strength, they started the huge barrel house rolling down the sand hill toward the sea. From inside the structure came the crash of tumbling furniture and the frightened wail of the rudely awakened little Mark. As the house careened down the hill, the door flew open and broke off at the hinges. Household furnishings began to spew out of the opening and down the hillside. The big barrel rolled faster and faster until, as it hit the surf line, it spun sideways and still more objects flew out of the door opening. Two of those flying objects were the twisting, kicking body of little Mark and the grayish-green ball of ambergris, both arcing through the air toward the deeper water to seaward.

All three of the watchers on the hillside made nearly simultaneous dashes for the surf, the robbers in pursuit of the ball of precious ambergris and Sal to overtake the more precious bundle of struggling, crying humanity.

Now, it happened that at the point where the large barrel hit the water, a rather large slough or underwater ravine cut at right angles into the sand beach. This made for good fishing, but it also made for the formation of dangerous rip tides, or races, flowing away from shore and directly out to sea. At this time, the tide was beginning to ebb and such a rip was forming, so both Mark and the ambergris were catapulted into the mouth of a boiling, surging current, and both were in imminent danger of being irretrievably lost.

Straight as a martin to her nest, Sal flew to the rescue of her son. Without a second's hesitation, she plunged into the menacing rip tide and caught him to her breast. Keeping her back to the beach, she dug her bare heels into the sandy bottom to brace herself and to fight the powerful suction of the surging water. Simultaneously, the two robbers reached the floating ball of ambergris, and both grabbed hold of it and pulled it and themselves under water. Not wise in the ways of the surf, they had no idea how to get out of the rip, so they were tumbled head over heels, sometimes on top of the water and sometimes underneath, as they tried to fight the strength of the current. Fighting both the ocean and each other for their prize, they were swept by the current far out to sea, beyond hope of rescue.

Sal's neighbors, alarmed by all this commotion, came running down to the beach. They first saw to the safety of the Wrack Woman and her boy. Then they quickly put out to sea in pulling boats to search for the robbers and, if possible, rescue them. Although they rowed back and forth and up and down the beach until long after daylight, their search was unavailing. The two bodies were to wash up on the beach some three days later, with no way of identifying either of them. They were given a Christian burial in the woods back of Diamond City. So far as is known, no trace of the ambergris was ever found.

By midday, the islanders had rolled Sal's house back up its sand hill to a position of more security. This time, they secured it so firmly that it would never again roll down the hill into the sea.

One day a black poodle with intelligent, twinkling eyes showed up as mysteriously as Sal herself and attached himself to the little family. He soon endeared himself to Sal and Mark, and he remained with them for the rest of his natural life. Sal named him Money and permitted him to move into the barrel house during the wintertime at the insistence of Mark, whose daylong companion he became. When he was full grown, the dog weighed exactly five and one-half pounds and was a bundle of inquisitive energy. He loved to go clamming with his little master and would dig furiously until he had uncovered a clam. When

Sal would haul in fish on her hand line, he was the very spirit of excitement, jumping about each fish and barking and nosing it ever higher up on the beach.

Money's chief pleasure, though, was to go with Sal and Mark in a borrowed skiff to sell fish in Beaufort and to see and smell the delights of that ancient coastal town. In those days, as in these, fish were weighed in metal wire baskets and were paid for by weight. All the seafood dealers used platform floor scales to weigh the fish as they bought them. It was a routine matter to swing a basket of fish up onto the platform, adjust the balance rod, and cry out the weight for the dealer to translate into dollars and cents. This was the way all the fishermen sold their catch, including Sal.

All was going well, and the dealers welcomed Sal until they began to notice a very peculiar thing about her fish. It seemed that, no matter which dealer Sal sold her fish to, that dealer would finish up the day exactly five and one-half pounds, or some multiple of that figure, short. Thus, he would wind up with five and one-half pounds of fish missing, or exactly eleven pounds missing, or sixteen and one-half pounds short. The dealers could not, for the life of them, find out why this should be so. The platform scales were checked and rechecked against known weights, and they were accurate to the ounce. But still the shortages continued. This was a comparatively minor nuisance, but it began to get under the hides of the dealers. They compared notes and found that they came up short only when they bought from the Wrack Woman.

Having established this clue, the dealers set a watch on Sal when she next showed up with fish to sell. Sure enough, the culprit was discovered. Every time Sal had a basket-ful of fish set onto the scales, Money would slip around and perch himself on the scales behind the fish, out of sight of the weighmaster. Thus he was weighed with each lot of fish, and his weight was paid for each time. Money was really living up to his name, and the dealers were so fascinated by the way he pulled it off that they did not expose him for a week or more. They calculated that the dog was sold as five and one-half pounds of fish at least a hundred times.

When confronted with this chicanery, Sal was horrified. She indignantly claimed that Money had thought up the whole deal himself. In the end, no refund was ever demanded or made, but from that time forth, Money was absent from the trips to Beaufort to sell fish. No one ever completely explained Money's affinity for those platform floor scales. The Wrack Woman vigorously denied that she had ever trained him in such an activity or that his name had anything to do with his slick dealings. Money, of course, had no comment.

When Mark was seventeen, he ran away to sea, for a war was going on at the time and high wages were being paid for the services of merchant seamen. Although his mother forbade it, he slipped away one day to the main-land and signed on as a merchant seaman by lying about his age. He had always been big for his age, and the deception went unsuspected or, at least, uninvestigated by the ship owners. He occasionally wrote Sal after that, and he always enclosed some money. His letters got farther and farther apart and finally stopped altogether. No one ever received word that he had been lost at sea, and so far as is known, he never came back to his childhood home, but Sal was always serenely confident that he was alive and well.

Sal grew lonely after Mark was gone. Most of the settlers at Diamond City had moved to Harker's Island, Salter Path, or the mainland, and neighbors were few on Shackleford Banks. Fishermen occasionally came by day, but they always returned home before nightfall. The men from Lookout Lighthouse checked on Sal now and then, just to see that she was all right, and sometimes a former neighbor would drop by for a visit. In the main, though, she was alone.

When visiting neighbors brought their children, the lonely woman would fascinate them with stories of the sea and the creatures in it. Her fame as a storyteller spread over the entire region. Her very mysteriousness and the unusual house she lived in, as well as her reputation for second sight, completely enthralled the youngsters. It got to the point that the mere promise of a visit to the Wrack Woman's house was sufficient bribe to influence a child to behave for long periods of time or to apply himself diligently to his schoolwork or most anything else his parents had difficulty in persuading him to do.

And what tales she would tell! She would point to the sparkling surface of the sound, ruffled by a gentle breeze at sunset, and tell the children how all that glitter came to be. "In all the years since man has sailed the seas," she would whisper, "there have been thousands and thousands of shipwrecks. And in many of those shipwrecks there have been precious gems. Diamonds, rubies, sapphires, and other beautiful gems of all colors and sizes have been lost forever and now lie at the bottom of the sea." Looking all around her with a conspiratorial air and speaking in an urgent, confidential tone, she would continue, "But not for always and forever! The King of the Sea has granted to those lost jewels the power to rise at sunset to the surface of the sea and, for one hour, to gleam and sparkle with all their fire and beauty. Theirs is the choice as to whether they shall appear on the surface of the ocean or of the sound, but their time is limited to one brief hour each day. This is so that man can, once again, see the beauty that he has lost. But never try to gather these beautiful, lost jewels," she would warn. "If you try, they will recede into the depths again, for they now belong to the King of the Sea. Mortal man can never again possess them. He may only look at them and marvel at their brilliance, as they shine for their appointed hour and then settle back into the huge jewel box of the sea."

The beautiful but dangerous Portuguese men o' war were not really jellyfish to her. They were the jewel-like hearts of mermaids who had been betrayed by reckless seamen. Filled with sorrow and the desire for revenge, they were more dangerous to touch than a serpent and were to be avoided at all costs. Their very touch, she warned, would bring severe pain and injury, maybe even death.

To many people this lonely lady living out her days in the weatherbeaten old hogshead seemed to be the very incarnation of the spirit of the sea itself. She was part and parcel of it, and it seemed no more strange to see her fish her antiquated hand line than it was to see an osprey make his familiar, thrilling plunge into the sea in quest of prey. She belonged as Lookout Light, Fort Macon, and Salter Path belonged.

One August, a falling barometer, as well as the weather knowledge of the old folks, foretold a terrific storm in the offing. On that same day, the keeper of Cape Lookout Light reported the longest line of porpoises he had ever seen. On and on they came, stretching almost from horizon to horizon, surfacing and submerging, surfacing and submerging and, in what seemed to be almost a single file, drawing an undulating brown line across the ocean as far as the eye could see. Such a sight can fill even the most cynical with a sense of wonder and awe. To the Bankers, used to strange and wonderful sights upon the face of the deep, it seemed portentous, ominous. It betokened something, that was for sure, and most of the coast dwellers remained edgy and ill at ease until the mystery was resolved.

When the Coast Guard checked on Sal that afternoon to warn her of the approaching storm, they found her house deserted and the door standing open. Everything in the house was in order, but the owner was just not there. They searched the area surrounding the quaint home but could find nothing, not even a footprint. Later that night they came back again, this time to warn her to get out and to offer to take her to safety, but again no Wrack Woman was to be found.

After the vicious storm struck the next morning, the crew at the lighthouse watched Sal's barrel house through powerful binoculars, but they saw no sign of movement of any kind. Porpoise Sal had just vanished. She was never seen again, at least not in human form. There was no sign of distress, and no body was ever found.

Genuine Outer Bankers, particularly those around Shackleford Banks, Core Banks, and Cedar Island, still speak occasionally of Porpoise Sal. They have only kind words to say for her, for she was never known to harm anyone in her entire stay on the Banks.

Sometimes, when the old-timers see long lines of porpoises lacing the surface of the sea, they will take up their binoculars to see if they can find the leader. If one that is almost white or of a definitely lighter color than the rest heads the line, the watchers will smile and nod their heads and murmur softly, "Good luck. Good luck."

They believe Porpoise Sal has returned to her own, and many say that she has brought them peace. Anyway, the porpoise people are hunted no more, and it is considered the worst kind of luck to harm one.

The Maundy Thursday Affair

If you think that mysterious and unexplained incidents are confined to the mists of the Dark Ages, consider this tale.

The year was 1810. The locale was the lively and prosperous coastal town of Wilmington, North Carolina. The American Revolution was over and done with, or at least we thought it was done with. Our new nation had settled down to a period of prosperity and increasing personal income and wealth. The shadow of the War of 1812 was not yet apparent to most people. The Indians were mostly peaceful and industrious. On the eastern seaboard, it was a time of peace and plenty.

In Wilmington, a group of young men, sons of wealthy families, had grown up and developed into hellions and rakes of the first order. This was the case in many seaport towns of the day. These young wastrels held nothing sacred above their own pleasure and believed in nothing other than their own cleverness. "Eat, drink, and be merry" was not just their motto; it was their entire way of life. These young hedonists devoured all the profane literature they could find in search of new ideas for their debauchery. Roman orgies were reenacted down to the most sickening detail. Nothing, absolutely nothing, was too depraved for them. The only requirements were that, whatever it was, it must be novel and daring.

One of the leaders of this loosely organized group was a handsome young fellow named Lector Daniels. His parents had given him that name, hoping that he might develop into a noteworthy teacher, as one of his ancestors by that name had done. As a student at the University of North Carolina, he proved his brilliance by attaining one of the highest scholastic averages ever recorded there. During his junior year, however, he was expelled after the worst in a series of debauched flings had finally exhausted the patience of school officials. Lector was sent back to Wilmington, where his father immediately made him a full partner in the family's shipping business. With few serious duties and all the money he wanted at his disposal, this young snob threw himself with gusto into a life of complete uselessness.

In the spring of 1810, this young wastrel par excellence dreamed up what seemed to him an inspiration of pure genius. The season of the Passover was approaching and, with it, the Christian observance of the Last Supper, one of the holy days at which it was his wont to scoff. Why not have a mock Last Supper of his own design! The spacious "Upper Room" of the city's most famous brothel would be an ideal stage for such a farce. This location and the atmosphere prevailing there should give glorious opportunity for the extemporaneous wit and repartee, the unashamed blasphemy of which he and his friends were so fond.

And what a guest list! It seemed as though Fate herself was on his side. There was big Peter Brinker, large framed, blond, and just a little stupid by Lector's standards. Still, he was a skilled fisherman and was just the man to be the butt of any rooster-crowing jokes they might be able to manufacture. Then there were the half-brothers, James and John Cooper, the worthless sons of one of the most powerful political figures in the State. Andrew, Philip, and Matthew were the real names of three cousins whose rivalry to see which one could consume the most rum was notorious over the entire city. The stories of their drinking contests were almost legendary, and most of them were true. There was no Bartholomew, Thaddaeus, Simon, or Thomas, but there would be suitable companions in blasphemy to take the places of these four disciples. Jules Thomas would have to do for Judas, and Jimmy Galbraith would go along as James, the son of Alphaeus.

And to take the part of the Christus? Who, pray tell, would be more appropriate than Lector himself? Was not Christ, Himself, frequently called Rabbi, meaning "Master and Teacher," by his disciples? And did not his own name, Lector, come from the Latin word meaning a religious reader or "Teacher"? Here was a delicious opportunity for an affair that would be the talk of Wilmington for years.

Preparations went ahead rapidly. With a perspicacity beyond their years, the planners sensed that it would be best not to tell the madam of the house the exact nature of the event, for fear she would not let them use her second-story banquet hall. In this, they had read their hostess aright; Belle, for all her complaisance and easy virtue, had a deep religious sense. She would never have been a willing party to what followed. Indeed, it was said that the horrible results of that event haunted her for the rest of her life.

By the morning of Thursday, April 19, 1810, everything was in readiness. The upper banquet hall had been waxed and polished until it shone almost with a light of its own. The crystal chandeliers were dusted and polished and fitted with new candles, and the long table at which the feast was to be held was covered with Belle's very best linen tablecloth. And the food! Not used to denying themselves anything their wealth could buy, the revelers outdid themselves in providing food and drink. There were whole roasted pigs with red apples in their mouths, pheasant, guinea hen, and wild turkey, not to mention huge roasts of beef with all the trimmings. Seafood was prepared by every known method and in gargantuan quantity. There was wine in abundance and strong Jamaica rum by the keg, as well as oceans of champagne and other spirits. It was to be as lavish a "Last Supper" as its model had been simple.

About nine o'clock that evening, the invited guests began to arrive, some in hansom cabs and others in cabriolets closed against the evening chill, their horses stepping out briskly with little plumes of steam puffing from their nostrils. By ten o'clock all thirteen of the friends were in attendance, most of them already in their cups to varying degrees. Each was apparently delighted with himself for what he considered his daring participation in such a clever charade.

Midnight came and passed, and the jokes and speeches grew more and more ribald as the dulled senses of the participants required stronger language, broader jests, and coarser subject matter to tickle their respective risibilities. The language used that night was the most foul and profane that had been heard even in the collective experience of the participants. Poor Belle, who had mistakenly anticipated that she would be a sort of hostess, could stand it no longer. Pleading a headache, she fled to the lower floors of the house and was not seen again that night.

Sometime between midnight and the dawn of that Good Friday, the climax of the celebration came about. Swaying widely as he rose to his feet with his wineglass in his hand, Lector, the Christus, a crown of woven smilax on his head, proposed yet another toast.

What that toast was to have been was never known. As Lector rose to his full height and raised his wineglass, such an expression of horror crept over his face that it instantly stilled the drunken clamor at the table and caused his companions to stare at him. Suddenly, Lector, apparently cold sober and with an expression in his eyes as though he had just looked into the very jaws of hell, crushed the fragile wineglass in his hand as if it were a scrap of paper. The red blood from his pierced hand spurted between his fingers and down onto the gleaming tablecloth, where it formed a little bright puddle before sinking into the closely-woven fabric.

The room was so silent that the sputtering of a candle at the far end of the room sounded loud and clear, and the blood dripping from Lector's hand beat a slow, majestic rhythm on the table.

The voice that issued from Lector's mouth did not sound like his voice at all. It had an evil, sinister quality with awful overtones of authority. Speaking each word clearly and distinctly and with deliberate, majestic cadence, as though each word was being emphasized by the slow pounding of the blood in that clenched fist, the voice intoned, "Dead—in—six—months." And again, "Dead—in—six—months."

With a terrified scream, holding his bleeding hand to the bosom of his white, lace-trimmed shirt, Lector ran from the room, down the broad stairs, and out into the cool April night. The other twelve looked covertly at

each other for a moment or two, exchanged brief, preoccupied words of parting, and hurried from the building.
Forgotten was their custom of walking in a group as they
dropped each fellow at his home. Instead, each young man
seemed to want to avoid the others, and so the crowd
quickly disappeared into the darkness.

It was exactly one week later that the first death occurred. Sensitive young Jules Thomas, who had been
included in the party because his name sounded the most
like that of Judas, was found hanging by the neck from
a rope affixed to one of the low, sweeping branches of
the huge live oaks around his home.

The next week, Peter Brinker's drowned body was
found floating in the shallows of the river near his home.
Peter, who was one of the strongest swimmers in the
whole area and one of the best and most experienced
fishermen, drowned! His small rowing boat, when found,
was not even overturned.

As the weeks rolled by, it was first one, then another.
Andrew was accidentally shot and killed while out hunting in the marshes, and the next week, Philip accidentally
fell on his dueling sword while practicing for an affair of
honor. A week after Philip's untimely demise, Matthew,
an experienced horseman and half centaur, was thrown
from his mount and killed instantly.

Lector was, of course, distressed by these deaths. He
was a changed and sobered man who looked and acted
most of the time as if he were in some sort of trance. He
left Wilmington after Matthew's death, telling no one
either why he went or where he was going. The deaths
continued after he left with a macabre regularity—one

death per week until, by the end of the twelfth week, all of the Maundy Thursday party, except Lector, were dead, either by their own hand or under most mysterious circumstances.

What happened to Lector was not revealed in Wilmington until the following Christmas season. The brigantine *Esther* returned to Wilmington on Christmas Eve after a seven-month absence. Her one-legged cook spent the night in a waterfront tavern, obviously doing his best to drink himself into unconsciousness. The liquor did not seem to have its usual effect on him, though, and his eyes continued to hold a most mysterious, haunted look. He was very much like some latter-day Ancient Mariner; and, from long experience with the ways of seafaring men, the hangers-on at the tavern anticipated that he had a tale to tell. They hung around as the old cook lubricated himself to the point where he had to start spinning the yarn or burst wide open.

In the colorful, halting, beautifully expressive idiom of the old salt water sailor, Cookie told how young Lector Daniels had appeared at the dockside in Wilmington that early June night as the *Esther* was about to set sail for the Indies and European ports. The mate was happy to sign him on and even granted his strange request that he be allowed to sleep up in the chain lockers, forward, rather than in the forecastle with the rest of the crew. A strange one, this Daniels. He kept mostly to himself and had little to say to anyone. Seemed preoccupied, he did, like he had something terrible on his mind that he couldn't get rid of. Did his work well, though, and made a satisfactory hand.

The Maundy Thursday Affair

Then, one night in late October, when the worst storm imaginable was raging and the little ship was pitching and tossing as though she would capsize any minute, young Daniels came down into the lamp-lit forecastle where all the sailors, with the exception of the helmsmen, were trying to sit around a table that was fastened to the floor. In that wildly pitching forecastle and under that swinging and banging lantern, Daniels retold the story of the blasphemous party and its disastrous outcome, not sparing himself, but fully admitting his part in the whole affair. As he finished his tale, once again there was silence in the little forecastle as the crew watched Lector with alert, suspicious eyes. Only the loud slapping of the sea against the skin of the vessel and the wild screaming of the wind could be heard. The hanging lantern suddenly dimmed as though someone had turned down the wick.

And then, once again in that strange, sinister voice with its awful overtones of authority, Daniels' mouth intoned, "Gentlemen—tonight—it—is—exactly six months—since —that—Good—Friday." The sailors sat rigid with amazement and wonder. That was not Daniels' voice. It was a voice that froze them in their places with an instinctive and awful fear. Not one of them moved—not a soul even came to his senses—as Daniels heaved a pitiful sigh, rose to his feet, and climbed the ladder to the wave-lashed, pitching deck of the *Esther*. They heard one long, high scream as he went overboard into the maw of the storm and then— nothing.

So far as is known, Lector Daniels was never seen or heard from again. At least, as the sailors like to say, not heard from by anybody on this earth.